THE
FAKE
MUSEUM

A Novel

Ronin Parker

187th Street Books
A Division of Toyns Publishing
New York

RONIN PARKER
The Fake Museum

.

Ronin Parker lives in Washington Heights, NYC. To receive a free Brady Dillinger novella or join the mailing list, visit his website at roninparker.com

You can sometimes find him on social media at @roninparker

187th Street Books, a TOYNS Publishing imprint | New York, NY

First I-S Edition: February 2023

To purchase copies of this book in bulk, please contact us by email at toynsbooks@gmail.com

187th Street Trade Paperback ISBN: 978-0-9970678-4-2

10 9 8 7 6 5 4 3 2

THE
FAKE
MUSEUM

ONE

I DON'T LIKE TO STEAL FROM MUSEUMS.

When I was a young boy, they were one of the few field trip destinations I could go to, since the admission was free—it didn't cost the school district anything to put me on the bus with other children. Most trips required a fee my mother couldn't pay, so I had to stay at the school, in the vice principal's office, or the library, wherever there was a spare adult to supervise me. And the Smithsonian was *always* free, even on weekends when there was no field trip, a place I could look at art or just go to warm up on days I was in the city, with my mom on one of her lunch dates trying to scrounge up another husband. I developed a soft spot for museums then, and as a result I generally try to steal only from businesses and corporations.

This museum was different though, so I didn't mind trying to rob it. You probably never even heard about the place before the heist put it in the news. The Lessaker Museum? Very few people knew it existed, at least until the burglary. But I'm getting ahead of myself.

How it came about was: I had to leave my old job, which

was managing a night school for would-be air conditioner repairmen in New York. After many years in the heist game, I had settled down for a steady paycheck with benefits and things like that.

I was actually pretty good at it—a lot of the students had criminal records and so I understood them, plus I have an eye for detail and organization, and I discovered it could be used to manage a school as easily as to rob a place. Although it turns out that robbing places pays a lot more, especially since the night school ran out of money and stopped paying its employees just before Easter.

"Sorry, we just don't have any money left," said Mr. Point, the accountant. "I thought we had more hidden away some-where, but we don't."

He shrugged his shoulders. He had looked sad the whole time he worked there and at least now his facial expression made sense. We never found out where all the students' tuition money had gone.

I decided to go out for a drink with Byron Soop, who taught commercial air conditioner installation, and Phoebe Garlic, the receptionist.

It was just us three that night. Somehow, the school's manager, Sid Tillessa, had notified the other staff and forgot to tell us. Plus, he had someone call the students and tell them class was canceled that week, but they should come back next week, when, presumably, they'd find the school abandoned, and locked, or maybe even with a new tenant in the space. They would all want refunds but there would be nobody around to provide them. Anyway, Byron, Phoebe, and I went to Kersey's Bar, one of the last dives on the West Side that hadn't yet reinvented itself to capture High Line tourists. We didn't invite Mr. Point.

Byron usually drank for free at Kersey's, a deal he worked out whereby he fixed their air conditioner whenever it broke, and they'd let him drink free for a few months. So he drank a lot in the spring and summer, then in the winter when he had to pay for his drinks, he stayed away, sobered up, and got back in shape, sort of a reverse hibernation. Meanwhile, a guy who knew how to repair old boilers like the one they had for heat did all the free drinking through the winter. Since we hadn't gotten paid that night like we expected, Byron kept going to the bar and getting free pitchers for us to share. We were about three pitchers in when we started talking about what we would do next.

"I might look for a job back in Maryland," Phoebe said. "You know I used to work at the front desk at the Peabody?"

"Never heard of it," Byron said.

"Byron ain't got no culture," I said. I didn't know what the Peabody was either, but I figured it had to do with culture, since I had never heard of it.

"It's a fancy music school," Phoebe said. "Like Juilliard. Or Berklee."

"Oh yeah, Juliet O'Berkeley," Byron said. "She runs a great music school." He was pretty drunk by this point—I think he may have already been a bit drunk when he showed up at the school earlier. He closed his eyes and fell asleep on his stool.

"What took you from a fancy music school to an air conditioner repair school?" I asked Phoebe.

"I followed a man to New York. We were gonna get married, and then he got arrested, and I had to get a job."

"What'd he get arrested for?"

"Murdering his first wife."

"Ouch. Guess you dodged a bullet there."

"Yeah, too bad for her, she didn't."

"You weren't involved, were you?"

"No, he had killed her a few years earlier. Then he went to Baltimore to lay low and that's when we met. I didn't know anything about it, and for some reason he never mentioned it.

He thought the police had forgotten about him, but when we went to the courthouse here in Manhattan to get hitched, the justice of the peace recognized him from a wanted poster. Lucky for me it was before the ceremony. So I'm still single."

I almost told her about my history as a burglar, but then Byron toppled over onto the bar. It seemed like a sign that we should go, since we needed to help Byron get home, and we couldn't get any more free pitchers now that he was passed out.

Phoebe helped me get him into a cab, then she waved goodbye and waltzed down to the subway. I hopped in the back of the car with Byron, pulled out his phone and pressed his thumb against it to unlock it, then found his address and gave it to the driver. We drove through the hazy spring air up to Washington Heights. We kept going, under the George Washington Bridge bus terminal, and into a neighborhood full of synagogues. Outside his building, I dug into Byron's wallet and paid the cab driver with the last of his cash. Passed out Byron, I hate to admit, did not have enough cash to give him a big tip.

The cab pulled away and for the third time that night, I dug into Byron's pocket, this time to get his keys. Luckily I know enough about locks that I didn't have to try every key on the keychain—I could identify which key went with which bolt and got us inside rather quickly. From the vestibule, I saw the building had a camera, but when we got into the lobby, I noticed it wasn't plugged into anything. A lot of these older buildings had set up non-functioning cameras to scare off neighborhood hooligans. Buildings with younger people in them were now installing cameras that used WiFi, but Byron lived in an old man's building. These are the kinds of things I notice when I enter a building.

Thankfully there was an elevator, so I didn't have to lug him up the stairs. The hallways were that mix of forest green and French vanilla that was popular sometime in the 1980s. All the woodwork was buried beneath a quarter inch of old paint, and every once in a while you could see through a chip or scratch the whole rainbow of previous paint colors, like when they cut a highway through the side of a mountain and you can see all the different layers of earth from the very beginning of time. After unlocking his door, I finally put his keys back in his pocket and dumped him on the couch. We didn't have the sort of relationship where I was going to tuck him into bed.

———

I ALMOST MISSED IT. If I'd just left him on the couch and beat it, I would never have seen it. But, nice guy that I am, I figured I should find him a glass of water and put it on the coffee table in case he woke up in the night. His bedroom door was open and I saw an empty glass on his nightstand. That seemed less intrusive than rifling through his kitchen cabinets, so I walked in and grabbed the glass, figuring I'd rinse it and fill it in the bathroom sink off of his bedroom. But when I picked up the glass and turned around, I saw the painting.

It practically jumped off the wall at me. I mean, I hadn't seen this specific picture before, but I'd seen ones like it. The artist was that famous guy, who painted kind of sloppily, and he hated women, which you could tell from looking at his art. People pay a lot of money for his stuff. I think he might have killed his wife or punched her friend or something, and maybe that's why rich people like his work so much, because of the violence and cruelty. They're horrible that way.

This painting in particular looked like it was painted with a butcher's knife instead of a brush. Slashes of red and black, streaks of yellow, daubs of white. From some angles it looked like a woman's face, but from others, it looked like a crime scene photo.

Don't worry, I didn't steal the painting—I filled up the water glass and walked back into the living room.

"Byron," I said softly.

He tried to roll off his stomach and failed.

"Mhhmmmbouy. Mmmft," he replied.

"Byron, I have to ask you something."

"Hurgggle. Purgggle."

I turned him onto his side.

"Byron, where'd you get that painting in your room? Is it stolen?"

"Nahhhhhh. Not solen. I dint sole it."

"Did you buy it?"

"Heh. No. Couldn afford it. Was a giff."

"A gift?"

"Fromma museum. I did all their AC. Vents. Fans… Vents. Did it all. Air Conditionering. Was me."

"You installed the air conditioning in a museum? By yourself?"

"Course I did. Big tough job. Took me almost a week."

"You installed the air conditioning in a museum in a week? Byron? And they gave you that painting?"

"Said they couldn't sell it, for tax reasons. But could give it as a gift. Worth more than they were gonna pay me. Good for everyone."

"And it's real?"

"Yeah, the painting's real. But the museum is fake."

TWO

THE NEXT DAY, LATE IN THE AFTERNOON, I ASKED BYRON TO meet me near the small lighthouse under the George Washington Bridge. He showed up, a bit hungover, squinting a lot and keeping his head down. He ate from a small bag of potato chips, the kind that has a girl who looks like Nancy from the comics as their mascot.

"Tell me more about this fake museum," I said. "Is it fake like the stuff in Vegas? Like a replica of the Guggenheim? A smaller version of the National Gallery?"

"No, no," he said. "It's not a copy of a museum. It's got its own building and art collection. The thing is, it doesn't really act like a museum. They don't want you to come look at the art. It's never open."

"What's the point, then? Why build a museum if you don't want guests?"

"There's the rub," Byron said. Then he took a bite of chips and chewed for a while. I watched a barge float by on the Hudson.

"It's a tax dodge," he said finally. "You know how rich people are always donating art to a museum? One of the reasons is, they like having their name on the wall next to the painting. Like it says the name of the painting, then underneath says, 'Donated by Big Dick Johnson's wife Esther' or some crap like that. But the other reason rich people like to donate art to a museum is that you get a big tax break because you're doing the public a kind of favor."

"Kids get to look at the art on a field trip, that sort of thing," I said, thinking of my childhood.

"Yeah, you get the picture." He nudged my arm so I was forced to pretend to laugh at his pun.

"The problem," he continued, "is that once you donate the art, you don't get to keep it. You want to look at the painting, you gotta go to the museum with all the other schmucks, even though it used to be your painting, or sculpture, or whatever."

"Can't they do a thing where they promise to give it to a museum after they're dead? That way they get to look at the painting until they croak, but they still get the tax break?"

"It's possible. But then their dumb rich kids don't get to look at the painting in private. Big Dick Johnson Junior has to go to the museum to look at his daddy's art collection once the old man kicks the bucket."

"It's tough being rich," I said.

"I wouldn't know. Anyway, what this one rich guy figured out—his name is Lessaker—is that he could start his own museum. Do all the paperwork, everything by the book, except he locates the museum in his backyard. And he limits visiting hours to one or two weeks a year, by appointment, for an hour. So like a hundred people a year ever get to go to this so-called museum. If anyone's even interested. The art is fine, but there's not much of it, nothing you can't see elsewhere, and it's real hard to get to. I think the only people that go are graduate students writing a paper about some artist he has on display, trying to impress their professor by seeing a painting that no one else can see.

"The scam part is that the rich guy, Lessaker, he's the chairman of the board of this museum, and he's got the keys, and it's in his backyard, so he can go look at his art whenever he wants. Or invite his friends over and show them around. He donated his entire collection to this pretend museum, so he got a ton of tax breaks, but he's also the only one who ever gets to see the art or show it to his friends and family. He gets to have his cake and eat it too."

A little squirrel ran up to us and stared at Byron's chip bag until he dumped the crumbs on the ground. The squirrel tried them but found them too salty and ran away again. Some pigeons, following after, thought the crumbs were just fine.

"It's like the Little Red Lighthouse over there," he said, pointing to the small structure. "It looks like a lighthouse, right? And technically, it *is* a lighthouse. Or it was, back when it was in New Jersey. Then they moved it over to the New York side. Only , it doesn't do what a lighthouse is supposed to do. Because the lights from the bridge mean you don't need a lighthouse for navigation if you're in a boat on the Hudson. So it's just for show."

"It looks nice," I said of the lighthouse. "Kids seem to enjoy it."

"Well, this Lessaker Museum … it looks like shit, and only *his* kids get to enjoy it. Nobody else. I tell you, I've seen warehouses that look nicer."

"And you installed the air conditioning? How'd you get that gig?"

"This Lessaker guy, his next-door neighbor, Fritz, collected old motorcycles. He built a fancy garage to tinker with them, and I installed the A.C. for him. Fritz and Lessaker talked at a polo game or yacht appreciation society or something like that, and he recommended me."

"Wait, so there's a backyard art museum right next to a garage full of vintage motorcycles?"

"Not really. They're next door neighbors, but their houses are three miles apart. Rich people have real big lawns."

"This is in Maryland?" I asked.

"Yeah, Potomac. Or North Potomac. I forget which." He turned to look at the Hudson. "You know, Brady, I never figured you for an art lover."

"Oh, I'm not much of one," I said. "But I think I'm going to rob this museum."

He didn't blink.

Nor did he gasp or turn away, and his eyes didn't pop out of his skull. He didn't cough sadly, or say "Gee whiz," or rub his chin. He didn't take out his cell phone and call the cops. Instead, Byron carefully considered the idea.

"We shouldn't spend too much time together, in that case," he said.

I hadn't really called him out to the lighthouse to ask about the history of the museum. I had spent all the previous night researching it online. But I knew if I tried to pull this job, I'd need an inside man, so I wanted to see what he thought of the Lessaker Museum, whether he was protective of it, or, as I hoped, resentful of the rich owners. When I was confident that he was no friend of theirs, I told him what I was thinking.

"You ever been involved in something like this?" I asked.

"I might have been, once or twice, maybe," he said.

THREE

THERE IS A VERY FINE LINE BETWEEN A CONSPIRACY AND, SAY, getting a group of friends getting together to look at blueprints for a bank vault while dreaming about the future. I don't know where that line is, I'm not a lawyer.

Suffice to say, I have it on good authority (a district attorney) that I have participated in several criminal conspiracies. It never felt like we were doing anything illegal—we were just a bunch of young people doing what young people do: drilling into a five-inch stainless steel door, triggering a lock mechanism with a coat hanger, opening the safe, removing all the cash and jewelry, then leaving as fast as we could in a precisely coordinated afternoon. Theft? Sure. Criminal conspiracy? It didn't feel like one at the time.

Like they say, crime is in the eye of the beholder.

A few years ago, a private consulting firm offered me a job testing the security of a number of wealthy men in Manhattan. Their clients were a mix of financial gurus and computer geniuses. They offered me good money, although in the way you do when you don't trust someone—in periodic installments. For instance, they'd provide me a luxury apartment to live in, but I wouldn't own it and they could throw me out if I did something that made them unhappy. My salary would have been fine, not huge, but I'd get a large bonus at the end of every year. They were hedging their bets against me taking all their money, finding a way into some millionaire's mansion, then robbing it myself.

But it wasn't just the money that would have kept me on a leash. These guys ran ops beyond providing personal security for the wealthy. They also hired out as support services to the armed forces. We used to call those kinds of people mercenaries, but now they're government contractors, and some of them even advertise during football games. In any case, I didn't doubt they had helped a few dictators vanish in other countries, and probably had their fingers in the surprise disappearances and tragic car accidents that killed notable Americans as well. Not the kind of people I wanted to rob or work for, so I turned down the job. If I'd taken it, though, I would have been doing things that *should* have been crimes but *weren't* because I would have been a *consultant*.

I have never met a consultant I could trust.

Which is all just a long way of saying that I'm less concerned with whether something is legal—which is just a point of view—than I am concerned with whether something is ethical. For instance, stealing a loaf of bread to feed your sister's children who are starving in France in the 18th century is a criminal act. But even if it were legal, you shouldn't do it, because it will lead to the musical *Les Misérables*, which is pretty awful and sung too often by insufferable theatre types. On the other hand, if you have a chance to push a health insurance executive in front of a lawn mower or a monorail, I think you have a moral obligation to do so, even if it's not technically legal.

You can probably tell I don't know too much about the law or about ethics. That's because I've never robbed an attorney's office or a philosopher's library. Neither of them has anything of value in it, as far as I'm concerned.

And when I say *rob*, I mean *steal*, because a district attorney explained to me once that "robbing" means using force or threatening to use force to take something, and I rarely use force, except to pry open a window or something like that. I use the words "robbery" and "stealing" interchangeably, I guess, because I never stole a legal dictionary that would have taught me the difference.

Most of what I know in this world I learned when I was planning one of my heists. I learned about stamps when I robbed the old man Franzetti, and I learned about comic books when I robbed the Hines family mansion. So now that I was going to rob a museum, it was time for me to learn about art.

But first I had to assemble my group of friends, which was, *I want to state for the record*, not a criminal conspiracy. Just some people who like to discuss hypotheticals.

To start with, I had to get in touch with Josie Price. She was always traveling to exotic locations between jobs so it was never easy to track her down. She was an art forger who often helped me with money situations, figuring out what to do with large amounts of cash, for example. But her day job was in the art world, and I thought she may be able to help with logistics. I didn't want to email her if I could avoid it, since that would create what we used to call a paper trail. I don't know what they call it now when there's no actual paper involved. I guess it's still a paper trail, because if you get caught, they print out the emails on paper to use as evidence in court.

I bought a disposable cell phone and called the number I had for her in Vermont. It rang a few times and then her machine picked up.

"Hello, this is Josie. I can't answer the phone just now, I hope you understand. Please won't you leave a message?"

There was some sort of jazz music with vibraphone playing in the background.

"It's me. Uh. I don't want to say my name. You know me, though, I hope. From my voice? If not, uh, I don't know. I'll figure something out and call you back in a bit. So I guess you can disregard this message."

Whoops.

I was out of practice, having worked that regular job at the air conditioning school for too long. Rusty. But planning a heist is a skill that always comes back to you, just like stealing a bike.

Half an hour later, I called back.

The jazz music played and Josie talked and then it beeped.

"Hi, it's me again. We caught the same train in Colorado once. Anyway, I'm into a new line of something. If you're around and looking for something to do, give me a call. I'm at, let's see, New York area code, the number of the apartment in Glendale, the number of cameras deactivated at the place in Miami, and Larry Bird's number. You know, the basketball player from the Celtics. So, uh, call me if you're interested. I'm just getting started so I don't have a timeline yet."

I hung up. A few minutes later, I called and left another message.

"Hi, this is Brady by the way. In case those messages were confusing. Brady Dillinger, the thief. Anyway, talk to you later, I hope."

FOUR

WHILE I WAITED TO HEAR BACK FROM JOSIE, I PAID A VISIT TO the Old Man in person. He had decided he only ever got bad news over the telephone, and threw his away. This was an old landline—he yanked the cord out of the wall and threw away the plastic unit, which may have belonged to the phone company given how long ago this happened. Suffice it to say, he never bought a cell phone.

He was living out his days in Leonia, New Jersey, in a nice big house, where a niece took care of him in exchange for rent-free living. I took the bus out from Manhattan because I didn't want to deal with parking, and it dropped me off a few blocks from his house. The walk was pleasant enough, through the suburbs on well-maintained sidewalks, and then I was at his door.

Standing there, about to ring the bell, I realized he had no way of knowing I was coming, and I had no way of knowing if he was home, or, honestly, still alive and not drooling in a retirement home or something like that. His niece probably had a cell phone I could have called, but I didn't have the number. So I wished for a little luck and rang the bell.

"Hold your griping horses!" I heard him yell from inside somewhere.

"Calm down, he only rang the bell once." I assumed this was the niece replying.

"Once is too much, I was reading!"

"You were sleeping with a book in your lap, you liar. I'm surprised you even heard the bell over your own snoring."

"Some day, Keisha, you'll be old like this, and I'll be looking up from hell and laughing at your troubles."

"Yeah right, you'll be sleeping in hell too, you lazy lump."

It was great to hear him bicker again.

Closer to the door, I heard Keisha say, "I'm going to open the door, Clyde."

"Wait, maybe they went away, a normal person should have rang the bell again, we've taken so long."

"It could just be someone polite."

"Then don't answer it, it must be a stranger, since I don't have any friends who're polite."

I rang the bell again.

"I thought I said to hold your griping horses, I'm coming," Clyde said, a little closer to the door it sounded like. "I'm not Jim Thorpe, you know."

Finally, Keisha opened the door.

"Hi, Clyde," I said.

"Oh, it's only Brady," he said to Keisha. "All this fuss for Brady. Make sure he doesn't take the silverware."

"Good to see you too, Old Man," I said.

"Come on in, I was just reading."

"Napping, he means."

"This is Keisha. She acts like she's my nurse even though she never went to nursing school and I don't pay her anything."

"Nurse! Ha! Start choking and see if I save you like a nurse would."

"I didn't say you were a good nurse, did I?"

We walked into his living room and he sat in a beat up old arm chair. He gestured to a brown Winchester couch and I sat down.

"Do you want Keisha to leave?"

"I wanted to talk business," I said and shrugged.

"Eh, she knows the business, don't you, Keisha?"

"I know enough to get you locked up if you sass me too much, Old Man," she laughed, and sat down next to me on the couch.

"I had to tell her everything so she wouldn't accidentally sell one of my stolen rare coins on the internet."

"Internet? No way. I'd go on *Antiques Roadshow*, become famous with your stolen coins and things. Meet Mark Wahlberg! Not the one who did hate crimes," she added to me, "the one who hosts the *Roadshow*. He also hosts *Temptation Island*, and I have a lot of questions about that series."

"Anyway, Brady, what brings you here?"

"I'm thinking about a job. It's the early stages, you know how that is."

"Do I ever. It's like going on a date. You start thinking, *Maybe she's the one.* You get your hopes up and everything. But the danger is, you start ignoring her flaws because you want to be in a relationship so bad. She chews with her mouth open, but she's so pretty you don't mind. She's rude to the waiter, but she laughs at your jokes. Pretty soon you're engaged, but you ignored the signs that she was a monster because you didn't want to be lonely."

"Pffft," Keisha said. "That's really old fashioned. These days, if you don't want to be lonely, you just find a hook-up with an app. Keeps your brain unclouded."

"Keisha loves her apps," Clyde said.

"I don't love them, I have a normal relationship with my phone and my apps, just like any young person. You have a fear of apps, because you're old and because you're a luddite."

"A luddite?"

"It means you hate machines and technology, I learned it from my word-a-day app."

"Anyway, I remember I once spent six months trying to figure out how to rob the off-hours poker game on 30th Street."

"The one the deputy commissioner played at?" I asked. "Wasn't it guarded by off duty cops and across the street from the precinct?"

"Sure, sure. But other than that, everything else seemed easy, so I kept thinking if I could find a way around the guards, it would be a clean score."

"Wishful thinking," Keisha said.

"If it had been further from the police station, I could have maybe found a way in during a shift change. But it was too close, so the bodyguards were always in the equation."

"You wasted six months, you could have spent that time helping orphans or visiting sick people at the hospital," Keisha said.

"Why punish those poor dying children?" Clyde said. "They don't want me visiting. Anyway, it wasn't a waste. Just like with women, that six months was full of possibility and hope. I could almost taste the money I was gonna get."

"That's about where I am now," I said. "It's all optimism and none of the real-world practical stuff bringing me down yet. That's why I'm here. I figured if anyone could talk me out of it, you could."

"You came to the right place, he hates everything," Keisha said.

"That's not true," Clyde said. "I don't hate criticizing you."

"Oh yes, you love criticizing me. I think it may be the only thing keeping you alive."

"Anyway, Brady, tell me what you got."

FIVE

I GAVE HIM A BRIEF DESCRIPTION OF THE MUSEUM. I WOULD have told him the details of the plan, but I did not have one yet.

"An art museum?" he asked. "That's a tough bag of pretzels. Putting aside security for a bit, you have to think about the press. Not just news coverage, which is fickle, but the arts pages would be all over that sort of thing. So you'll be stuck with some hot paintings everyone will recognize."

"He thinks people still read newspapers," Keisha said.

"Newspapers, blogs, whatever they're reading. Tweets? Is that right?"

"That's right," Keisha said. "I guess you're not as senile as I thought."

"Anyway," Clyde said, "you have to be ready for that media saturation."

"My idea about that," I said, "is to figure out a way to make it clear this Lessaker fellow was the bad guy, hoarding important art in his mansion, no security, not really letting the public see it."

"I like that," Keisha said. "Everyone is sick of super rich dudes, with their yachts and spaceships."

"Fine," Clyde said. "But you still gotta think about how the attention will affect sales. Hot art is a hard sell on the black market. People buy art for three reasons. Because it's an investment, because they like it, or because they want to impress someone who likes it.

"The investment buyers are out of the picture in this case, no pun intended. Stolen art is a bad use of money because you could be charged with a crime for buying it, and on top of that, you can never resell it in public without it getting returned to its original owner."

"You're a fountain of joy," I said.

"It's just the truth, kid. So where was I? Oh, yeah, then we're left with people who buy it because they like it, or because they want to impress someone who likes it. In both cases, the art actually has to be good, which rules out most of the paintings from the past hundred years. You know, lobby art."

"Like that collection of beach chairs!" Keisha said.

"Oh, don't remind me of that crap," Clyde said.

"We went to some building in the city for one of his blood tests, and in the lobby, hanging on the wall, is just a bunch of folded beach chairs. I asked the guard at the sign-in desk, were those chairs for people who had to wait in the lobby during the summer? He said, no it was a five million dollar work of art, called 'Urban Beach.' I told him I could have saved him five million bucks and bought the chairs at the thrift store."

"They didn't want to save money though," Clyde said. "You know they got these laws where you have to spend like a tenth of a percent of your building's budget on public art. These construction companies are lazy, so they'd rather buy one big five-million-dollar piece of art for the lobby than buy hundreds of smaller works by other artists, which means they inflate the price of the shitty art."

"It wasn't even art," Keisha said. "Didn't make you feel anything or think anything. It was just there."

"That's the point, too," Clyde said. "They don't want someone coming into the building complaining that a mural is racist or homophobic or communist, so they buy the blandest stuff they can find for as much money as they have to spend, eat all their cabbage in one sitting."

"How was your blood work?" I asked.

"Fine. The doctor says I'm going to live to be 900 years old, like Noah. Getting back to your idea, though, that means you need to steal art that people actually like, specifically rich criminals. A rich do-gooder isn't going to risk buying stolen art, like I said, because it could get them in hot water, even with their elite lawyers and crisis management teams. They commit white-collar crimes, but they don't want to risk real jail time. That means you're selling to people who don't mind breaking the law, like gangsters, pimps, or musicians. Can you find one of them who loves contemporary art so much they'll pay for a bunch of pictures of mops or pools or lady parts?"

"The only musician I know is the guy who plays piano at Muldoon's during brunch. I don't think he's very rich."

"What about gangsters or pimps?" Keisha asked.

"Well, now," I said. "I don't know any pimps. I'm not even sure they still exist in the world, with the internet and everything. I have been acquainted with a few gangsters, but I don't think any of them were the art appreciating type."

"What sort of art do they have on display right now at this museum?" Clyde asked.

"I can check," Keisha said, picking up her phone from the coffee table.

"Is that safe? We don't want a record of us looking up the museum our friend is going to maybe rob."

"It's probably fine," I said. "But just to be paranoid, I looked up the information online at a library, but not the one near my apartment."

I took out the small tablet of paper I always kept in my pocket, and flipped through to the right pages.

"Let's see, they got, 'Fierce Invocations: Women Without Men 1970-2016.' That's, uh, what it sounds like. Female artists who weren't associated with male artists."

"Why do they have to say 'without men'?" Keisha asked. "Doesn't that imply that they should have had men?"

"You'd have to ask the curator," I said. "Who is the rich guy's wife."

I flipped a page.

"Also on view is 'The Nautical Made Whole: Sculpture From Within 20 Miles of Water, 1997-1998.'"

"Very specific. Too bad sculptures are hard to steal," Clyde said. "Unless they're small. Maybe there's some nice driftwood pieces or something?"

"No, it's mostly giant metal lumps. And finally," I said, "they are showing 'Days in the Desert, Nights in the City: Caravan/Morocco.'"

"That's probably your best bet on the secondary market. Middle Eastern artifacts and things, you can probably find a collector out there who wants that stuff."

I flipped the page of my notebook. "Um, it's a three hour video of a naked guy rubbing spices on himself with a horse in the background."

"Probably not worth stealing. Unless you could get the horse. I'm sure somebody would want a horse."

"I'm not a cattle rustler," I said. "But those are just the current exhibitions. They also have a permanent collection, which is the main thing to go after. A lot of the temporary exhibits are on loan from actual museums, and I don't want to steal from a real institution."

This was another part of the scam I discovered. In addition to getting to keep his private collection while still getting a tax break on it, Lessaker used his fake museum to borrow works from legitimate institutions. So instead of going to some other place to look at art, he could have it shipped to his backyard for a while.

"I can put you in touch with a secondary market contact of mine," Clyde said, "but don't get your hopes up. Like I said, the art world's difficult. It's like trying to sell honey in the bear cage—it's dangerous and the bears don't have a lot of money, because they're bears."

I stood up as if I was ready to go.

"You can't leave so quickly," Clyde said.

"Oh, I thought I was intruding maybe."

"We should have offered him coffee. I told you we needed coffee!" Keisha said to Clyde. "His doctor," she said to me, "told him he had to quit drinking coffee. But he couldn't control himself. When I was asleep, he'd sneak down in the middle of the night and make himself some of my coffee, the idiot."

"I'm old, I should be allowed to do whatever I want at this age."

"Anyway, he said the only way he would stop is if we didn't have any coffee in the house, so we don't have any."

"I'm surprised he doesn't break into the neighbor's house and steal theirs," I said.

"I tried. They got a mean dog."

"Let me, for a special occasion, pop into town and buy some," Keisha said.

"How about just you two go to that trendy place and drink coffee there so you don't bring any back to the house and tempt me. I could use a nap anyway."

He hustled us out of the house, and we started walking

towards the main thoroughfare. For a while, we walked in silence.

"Didn't you go straight for a while?" she asked.

"I tried. But it turned out my employer was incompetent or a criminal. Or maybe both? They went out of business, and that was that."

"Clyde keeps saying I should study for a real job. I took a few classes, but I'm not sure I want the same thing he does."

"We used to fantasize about being CEOs with corner offices. He probably wants that sort of life for you."

"I'm not cut out for that shit. Plus, executives are even more dishonest than thieves."

We stopped talking for a bit as we walked by some children at a bus stop.

At the end of the block, I said, "The world is changing, and there's a lot more surveillance, cameras, things like that. You can't just cut a wire and make the cameras go off. Sometimes there's a guy in Mumbai watching the security feed through the internet. I don't even understand how it works myself. Maybe Clyde is just worried that the knowledge he could pass on to you wouldn't be helpful."

"I get it," she said. "It doesn't hurt to keep taking those classes, learn job skills I can put on my resume."

"Nursing?" I asked.

"I don't have the bedside manner for that. I've been studying computers. Specifically, encrypted data networks and packet transfer protocols. You know, the kind of thing people use to set up security cameras on a wireless network and stream the video to Mumbai."

SIX

It seemed like there was more to Clyde's niece than I realized. I had been worried she was some sort of wilting flower, sacrificing the best years of her life to take care of an old family member, the kind of woman who would end up a spinster, or whatever the modern, polite term for a spinster is. Cat lady?

But no, she was clearly aiming to get into the game some day.

"So, um, it's not a coincidence that you're learning that sort of computer stuff?"

"No. I realized it wouldn't be enough to learn from Uncle Clyde about his methods, since they were a little, you know, old fashioned. That's when I started getting into back-end computer analytics."

"They cover that kind of stuff at the community college?"

"Hell no, I'm getting my PhD in asymmetric security data collection at Rutgers."

"Sorry! I thought Clyde said you were taking a few classes at the local college."

"I am. It's 45 minutes away."

Inside the coffee shop, we ordered at the counter, then took our drinks to a table in the corner, far from other patrons.

"Why all the secrecy?" I asked. "Does Clyde really not want you getting into his line of work?"

"It was a decision we both made. I didn't want to just inherit jobs because he was my uncle and become some sort of nepotism thief. On top of that, he wanted to make sure it was really something I was choosing to do, and that I wasn't just falling into it out of laziness."

"Getting a PhD out of laziness?"

"It happens. A lot of my classmates, actually, are just kind of good at coding but don't really have a passion for it. Tons of people end up in academia because they get put in school when they're a little kid and then 16 years go by and it's the only thing they know how to do, so why not stay on that train?"

"I got kicked off the train. My college suspected me of stealing rare books from the special collections library."

"Did you do it?"

"No. Not at first, anyway. It was an old German professor named Rhinehart. They found the books in his house when he died. But after I was expelled, since they already thought I was a thief, I *did* break into the library and stole the college's original charter."

"They must have been furious."

"They still don't know I have it."

She took a pen out of her purse and wrote something on one of the small napkins, then slid it over to me.

"The college knew you under this name, right?"

She'd written down my real name.

"Not bad," I said, tearing up the napkin. "But Clyde could have told you that."

"He would never rat you out like that, even to me. You

know, growing up, I always thought Brady Dillinger was your real name. I didn't even think it was weird when I found out you were a thief, that you had the same last name as a famous bank robber. Recently I was trying to clean up Clyde's digital footprint and came across some connections to that name you just tore up, so I did a little digging and realized it was you."

She took out her phone, swiped it with her finger a few times, pressed a few buttons, and showed it to me. It was just green text on a black screen.

"Looks broken," I said.

"It's a command line app. Before, at the house, I wasn't going to leave a trail looking up the museum on my phone. I was bouncing signal through different houses in the neighborhood to make it untraceable."

"That's a neat trick."

"Not as hard as it seems. Most people in the suburbs use the password assigned with the router from the cable company. It's printed on the bottom of the box, so I get invited to their house once, for a Christmas party, pretend to drop something near the TV, take a look at the bottom of their router, and then I can log into their WiFi.

"Wouldn't they just give it to you?" I said. "You're an invited guest."

"I lied about the Christmas party. I might have snuck in while they were out of town on vacation."

"You broke into your neighbor's house?"

"Not to take anything, just for practice. Maybe my uncle was evaluating my skills."

"Maybe."

"And maybe more of our neighbors should invite us to their holiday parties so we don't have to break into their homes. Here's the thing. Uncle Clyde and I agreed I would find my own first job, not rely on any of his contacts or connections. Then you showed up at the house, and you needed his help. But it seems like you also need my help."

"Maybe," I said again.

"That's why he got us to leave, so I could ask you to let me in on this if I wanted to. He didn't want to ask on my behalf." She looked right into my eyes. "Let me be part of this."

"Maybe," I said once more, because I couldn't think of anything else to say, and it had worked the last two times.

"Okay, you can think about it for a minute."

She drank her coffee and fiddled with her phone for a bit. I drank my coffee and thought about it for the allotted minute.

I trusted Clyde, and she was his niece. On the other hand, he wasn't exactly recommending her. Maybe I should ask him about her sometime when she wasn't around? Added to the mix, my usual tech guy was still in jail in the Bahamas for fraud due to a fake music festival he'd helped organize.

"How do I know you're good?" I asked.

"Give me a second," she said, not looking up from her phone. Then, a few seconds later, she smiled and showed me her phone.

On the screen, there was a picture of me, taken from above, standing at the counter of the coffee shop about 20 minutes earlier.

"Shit," I said. "You're hired."

"Don't be too impressed, they have a weak security system here."

"No, no, you've got the job if you want it. Can you delete that picture though?"

"I can delete it from my phone," she said. "Not from their camera logs. At least, not using my phone. I can come back tomorrow with my laptop and take care of it."

"Delete the whole day's footage?"

"That'd be too suspicious. I'll probably clone yesterday's

footage and rename the file so they have two copies of yesterday and nothing from today. That way they wouldn't notice a file is missing until it's too late. Assuming they even have a separate back-up, but I doubt it. It's a mom-and-pop shop, not a corporate place. They probably bought something off the shelf at CostCo."

Having finished our coffee, we walked back to Clyde's house.

SEVEN

"SHE'S IN, RIGHT?"

"Yes," I said. We were in his living room, which was now covered in battered notebooks and some blueprints. The Old Man hadn't been napping after all, but going into his archives to see if he had anything that might be useful while we were at the coffee shop.

"First, here's a list of contacts that may be helpful."

He handed me a sheet of paper. Handwritten at the top was "Bird Watching Group." Then, below that, was a list of names and phone numbers.

"If something goes wrong," he said, "and police get involved, search your apartment, they'll ignore that piece of paper because bird watching is boring as all get out."

Keisha came back down from her bedroom, dressed in workout clothes.

"I'm going to the gym," she said.

"Show off," Clyde said.

"Don't start any conspiracies without me!" she whispered just before she left through the front door.

Clyde sat down on the couch and picked up a model rail-roading magazine.

"This one is pretty interesting, although you probably know all about it," he said as he handed it to me.

The cover of the magazine said "17 Tips for Mountain Top Trees" and "Are You A Tunnel Fanatic?"

Clyde may have overestimated my interest in choo choo trains, I thought. But I opened the magazine and a bunch of news clippings fell out. They were all about the Gardner Museum.

"I try to keep anything that might be considered evidence buried under the trappings of boring old man hobbies," Clyde said. "I've been subscribing to that magazine for years, but I've never actually read the darn thing."

Picking up the news clippings, I said "Wasn't the Gardner Museum heist a messy job? They suspected the mob, right?"

"It was amateur hour, for sure. But they've never been caught, so cheers to the amateurs."

In 1990, men dressed as police officers robbed the Isabella Stewart Gardner Museum in Boston. They tied up security guards and—what marked them as beginners—cut a bunch of paintings out of their frames. While you may resort to that in a time crunch, like the school teachers who stole a de Kooning from an Arizona museum a few minutes before it opened in 1985, the Gardner thieves had all night and could have treated the art better.

"Two things have always struck me as strange about that Boston job, as unnatural as unfrosted donuts," Clyde said. "One: It looked like a smash-and-grab, but maybe the clumsy, violent crime was covering up a smaller, more delicate crime."

That was a common trick in our business. Complete a professional job, but cover your tracks by making it look unpro-fessional. That way the authorities wasted time looking for local dope fiends or troubled youth, not realizing the whole operation was just to grab one valuable piece of jewelry that got lost in a long list of stolen items.

"Something similar happened in Mexico that we'll circle back to," Clyde said. "The second thing about Boston is: Was it two different robberies that just happened to overlap?"

"You're saying somebody stole a bunch of paintings the same night that someone stole…"

"Two small sculptures. Or the Manet, which was in a completely different room."

"I don't know," I said. "Just by coincidence, two different thieves target the same museum on the same night? That seems unlikely."

"It could happen. Especially if there was a day they were particularly vulnerable. In this case, the night of St. Patrick's Day, when the whole of Beantown was populated by thousands of thoroughly sauced nincompoops."

"I thought that was every night in Boston," I said.

"It's worse on holidays. But it wouldn't have to be a coincidence. It could be one smart set of thieves taking advantage of some morons. Let them think they were running the show while running a small job unnoticed in the background."

"So you think I could find some stooges to run a ham-fisted burglary of the Lessaker Museum while I sneak in and out more intelligently?"

"I don't know, Brady. It may be hard to find someone stupider than you. In your case, you may have to be the klutz, while a more intellectual type pulls off a simultaneous job."

"Thanks."

"Play to your strengths, I always say."

I thought about it for a while.

"It sort of amounts to the same thing, right? Either one thief pretending to be worse at his job than he is, or a thief hiding behind someone worse at the job committing a similar crime."

He handed me another model railroad magazine. This one said "Engineers: Mustache or Beard? We Asked 50 Top Modelers" and "25 Must-Have Diesel Engines for 2013."

Stuffed inside it were articles about the Mexican Museum of Anthropology, which was robbed on Christmas Eve in 1985. In that case, it was a couple of local college dropouts, but they had done such a precise job that the authorities assumed it was an international syndicate or some other experienced professionals. They spent months investigating false leads in the wrong direction because they overestimated the criminals. I looked at the article some more, wondering what he wanted me to see.

Then I figured it out.

"Both Mexico and the Gardner job happened on holidays, Clyde."

"You noticed! It's a good time to get away with something. First, the normal guards and police are often on vacation or using sick days, so you have less experienced fill-ins and rent-a-cops minding the fort. And on top of that, there's the general noise of standard holiday misbehavior, drunks, parties, music, feasts, maybe even fireworks. It gives people reasons to ignore suspicious things they might otherwise call the police about.

"And you know who's the worst about it? Rich people. They go to fancy galas and have fun and think to themselves that everyone in the world has the night off and is celebrating like they are. They forget there are people working, waiters and bartenders, their nannies, event staff … little people, poor people. They always end up working on holidays because they need the money, even if they would rather be spending the day with their family."

I put the articles back in his model railroad magazines and handed them to him.

"It seems too obvious to try Christmas or St. Patrick's Day again," I said. "Halloween could be fun."

"You get a lot of masks, but there's also a bunch of kids out and about. That could cause complications."

"Easter?"

"No one celebrates Easter anymore," Clyde said. "Especially not modern art enthusiasts. They're mostly atheists."

I knew he had a date in mind, but figured I could tease him a bit.

"Labor Day?"

"Never work on Labor Day, it's an affront to unions."

"What about Memorial Day?" I asked.

"That would be disrespectful to the armed forces, plus it's too hot in the summer, you don't want to be working hard then."

"Presidents Day?"

"Now you're just messing with me," Clyde said.

I smiled. "You're thinking New Year's, aren't you?"

He nodded. "It's perfect. Everyone's drunk, it's loud, and there's one other thing I like about it. You say this Lessaker guy is a tax cheat, right? That's why he has this museum?"

"That's what it seems like," I said.

"These types, they have accountants who figure everything out for them, down to the last detail. They don't wait until April 14 to do their taxes. Some brain in a suit is advising them at the end of the year on the best way to minimize their taxes. They figure out what donations and write-offs and business purchases they need to make in the last week of December. The government even helps them—I had a neighbor who bought a big SUV because they could deduct the whole thing as a business expense. He was complaining he would have rather bought a smaller car, but there was a tax loophole if he bought something over a certain weight, it was a sop to Detroit, to try to goose their sales. Now he's got a giant Chevy Suburban gas guzzler he hates driving."

"Sounds like he's got a rough life," I said.

"The point is: you do the job New Year's Eve, finish before midnight and make sure it's reported to the authorities on December 31, he won't be able to profit off the loss the way he might if his accountants had more time to work it out. You rob him in June, he's got six months to figure out how to cook the books to make money off it. If the burglary happens on the last day of the year, he's just got to suck it up and take it. That could throw off his whole tax picture. Sweetens the deal for you, puts some sugar in your chewing gum."

I thought it through for a bit.

"You got any New Year's plans, Clyde?"

EIGHT

LET ME TELL YOU THE STORY OF MALCOLM LESSAKER AND HIS fortune.

Like many of the rich, he says he is a self-made man. The tale he tells is a common one: a young man armed only with an idea cobbles together some money and starts a company. The business grows over time and, along the way, helps people, and, well, golly, the next thing you know the guy is a billionaire who hides his money in off-shore account, underpays his taxes, and hires illegal immigrants to look after his stable of thoroughbreds, with kids he hates away at boarding school, on his third wife, probably a nurse from his plastic surgeon's office or a former pageant runner-up, eating some new trendy diet he hates, wondering why he can't, with all the money at his disposal, find a decent solution for his baldness. You've seen these guys—they own football teams or try to buy elections out of pure vanity. You want to smack 'em but you know they'd sue you for all you're worth.

Malcolm Lessaker, to get back to specifics, came from money. He is actually Nicholas Malcolm Lessaker III, but obviously it's hard to pretend you came from nothing when you've got Roman numerals after your name. So he claims he's been called Malcolm Lessaker since his school days. The thing of it is, even that's a lie. In his Georgetown Preparatory yearbook, he is called Nicholas in every photo caption, and there's even a joke on the polo team page about him getting mad when he is called Nick rather than Nicholas. And he's quoted several times in the Duke student newspaper from his undergraduate years, always as "Nicholas Lessaker III." (Most of the articles were about some racist/sexist tradition that was being eliminated, and he was the one speaking up to defend it.) He used his name all throughout childhood, is the point.

And what a name it was. You're probably familiar with the Lessaker family, but just in case you're not, here's their story: Nicholas Lessaker père actually did come from nothing, or close to it. In 1909, his immigrant parents settled into Montana, believing the false promise of railroad companies that it was fertile, welcoming land. By the time he was 15, the homesteaders had mostly given up, leaving behind only dirt and barbed-wire fences. His mother had died and his father was wasting away, hoping for a miracle that would never come. Nicholas Lessaker I followed the railway east and eventually made it to Pittsburgh, where the railroad's steel came from, then traveled back out to Minnesota where the iron ore that made the steel came from, ending up in the Mesabi Range near Lake Superior. Here, during a labor strike in 1913, he somehow acquired a patent for a metallurgical process that helped make railroad spikes but became more important in building weapons for the Great War. Some say he bought the patent from a drunk scientist for mere pennies. There are also rumors that sex and blackmail were involved in the transaction. In any case, he took the patent to Washington, D.C., where he lived off it for almost a decade while he built his business port-folio. He was an enthusiastic supporter of America's entry into World War I, not for humanitarian or democratic reasons, but merely because he knew it would make him a wealthy man. And he was right. By Armistice Day in 1919, the penniless Montana drifter had become a wealthy homeowner, settled into a fieldstone mansion in Chevy Chase, a neighborhood he chose because he agreed with the views of the city's white supremacist founder, Francis G. Newlands. He was just 23 years old. Soon, he began to look for a wife.

Of course, since he already had money, he was looking mostly for a woman with pedigree. Perhaps a descendent from a Mayflower family, or a Daughter of the American Revolution. He wanted those connections to high society that would otherwise be withheld from a newcomer like himself, with his dirty industrial money. Honorable fortunes, in those days, came from the exploitation of people, not the application of science. But he was wealthy. The women came to him. Or, more precisely, their fathers and mothers did. Families who had fallen, or were barely clinging to their lifestyles: plantation owners, Philadelphia elite who had invested in financial swindles, ex-tycoons with gambling problems, as well as, from abroad, nobility struggling to stay afloat in the new Twentieth Century. Nicholas Lessaker enjoyed a parade of eligible young women of distinction who could elevate his status into stately strata.

And then he married a working girl. Not a prostitute, to be clear, but a woman with a job, which meant a commoner in those days. Lizzy Humboldt sold ladies' hats at a small shop in Georgetown. Lessaker was at the store to buy a gift for a countess from the soon-to-be-independent nation of Estonia. But he liked Lizzy's pluck and independence. He was more wowed by ambition than heritage, and certainly she was a comely figure. History does not tell us whether the girl from Estonia ever got her hat. That she did not get her man, we know for sure. Lizzy and Nicholas were married in February 1920. She never put on the trappings of wealth and never called herself Elizabeth. She had been born and raised a Lizzy, and she would die a Lizzy.

And while she did not bring prominent ancestors nor a country club membership to the table, she did help diversify her husband's holdings. While he expanded his ownership of various metallurgic processes that would profit from the second World War and ensuing Cold War, she moved some of their money into the retail business, which put a nicer face on their fortune, a family of textile merchants being more welcome at parties than a man who makes war machines.

One thing I forgot to mention about Lizzy is that she already had a son, Morris Humboldt. His father, her husband, had died in the Argonne Offensive several years earlier, just as the first World War was coming to an end. The reason Lizzy had a job was because she was a widow trying to get by on a tiny pension. It would be lovely to report that Nicholas Lessaker took in the boy and raised him as his own, but, alas, he was put up for adoption a week before the wedding, so that Lizzy could enter the marriage unencumbered, ensuring that the Lessaker fortune would go only to actual Lessaker offspring. Goodbye, young Morris!

Lizzy and Nicholas had five children of their own, of which the important one, for our purposes, was Nicholas Malcolm Lessaker II. As a child, unlike his parents, he never wanted for anything, except, possibly, their love and affection. They sent him away to school when he was five, just as the market crashed. The Depression does not seem to have affected the Lessakers terribly. Maybe one year, young Nicholas received only one gift horse when in better times he might have received seven or eight ponies. History does not tell us. He turned 18 when World War II was in full swing, but his money and connections kept him away from any real danger. Instead, he dabbled in the nascent intelligence industry growing up around Washington, D.C., mostly as an assistant to actual power brokers. His twenties coincided with the post-war boom, and he enjoyed his first marriage to a woman who does not figure into our story. He had the relatively common experience among the wealthy of dipping his toes into the waters of liberal causes and politics when he was young, before settling into miserly conservatism in his later years. In 1960, after divorcing the charitable do-gooder he had spent nearly two decades with, he married his second wife, a young woman with no such determination to help anyone but herself. This was the mother of "Malcolm Lessaker," who was born in 1964. As mentioned previously, he was born Nicholas Malcolm Lessaker III and showered with all the wealth and privilege the grand family could muster.

Perhaps it was in recoil from the disco glamour and glitter of the '70s that Malcolm leaned towards conservatism early. Or perhaps he found in Ronald Reagan an intellectual idol. Whatever the reasons, Malcolm never went in for liberal causes, except for the arts, but only then because he could put his name on the institutions and walls of galleries and museums.

He made his money off the sick.

That's right: He was not content to live off the Lessaker fortune. He started his own business in the health services industry. And he was good at it. He invented several new ways to make medical bills confusing. He innovated ways to charge the government multiple times for the same thing. He did not discover any cures, but when other, better people did, Malcolm made sure to get his finger in the pot and profit off of their hard work. There is a tradition of using leeches in medicine, and Malcolm was the biggest leech of them all.

The pinnacle of his career was the 1991 purchase of a small Florida pharmaceutical company, TravMG, that had patented a specific type of opioid that released slowly into the body. Like his grandfather before him, Malcolm took someone else's patent and ran with it. TravMG had no luck breaking into the market and getting clinical trials approved for their drug, but once Malcolm threw the weight of his health services companies behind it, the doors opened and tons of addictive drugs flowed through them. Probably some of your favorite celebrities have struggled with this opioid. Its incredible success ensured that Malcolm would never have to work again. And so he began his new hobby: hoarding wealth.

If he had taken his billions of dollars and become a philanthropist, I would have no desire to steal from him. But he used charities as a cover to keep more of his money from the government. The only people to benefit from his largesse were him and his accountants. For instance, he started a horse rescue society that took in horses whose owners could no longer afford them or were mistreating them. Instead of teaching the horses to work with sick children, though, he had them brought to his estate where they were trained to ride proper English style. This was called *rehabilitation*. Then they were sold, at below-market value, back to Lessaker, who added them to his stable. The money from the sale went back into the horse society, which used it to scour the country looking for more horses. They soon stopped looking for mistreated animals, which were harder to retrain, and focused on finding horses whose owners had fallen on hard times, then whisked those animals away. Essentially, he was a horse thief.

After that, he got into art collecting, which is a nice hobby for boring people. Part of it was probably the fact that he met an art dealer who was young and attractive, and buying art was an excuse to spend time with her. He spent a lot of time with her, so he ended up with a lot of art. Whenever she told him to buy something, he threw down his money and took it home. But you can only store so much art on the walls of your house, even if it's an enormous mansion. And you can't just put a bunch of valuable paintings into a storage unit with a padlock.

You have to put them into climate controlled storage at a place like Crozier's. Malcolm Lessaker looked at how much he was spending on art storage every month and decided there had to be a better way. This is when he realized he could start a non-profit museum and write off all the fees as charitable donations. But he didn't want to give away the art he had bought. So he put the museum in his backyard.

The Lessaker Museum sits on the acreage behind Lessaker's overcompensating mansion in suburban Maryland, far enough from Washington, D.C., to discourage tourists, but close enough for Malcolm and his wife to consider themselves power elite of the nation's capital.

He had to buy off several city councilors to get approval for the project, then made several large donations to Postal Service regulators to get his estate's address shifted from Travilah into the fancier-sounding North Potomac enclave, where it could almost pass for true Potomac (sans "North").

Now I don't claim to understand how rich people think. At this point, Malcolm Lessaker had more money than he could spend before he died. Why bother going to all this work to save a couple thousand dollars a month? That's just the way rich people are, I guess.

To pull off this job, I realized I would need someone who could move in the same circles as people like Malcolm. Somebody who understood the rich. So I called Fiona.

NINE

FIONA THE GRIFTER LIVED IN A SoHo LOFT WHERE SHE DIDN'T pay rent.

When I first met her, she was living on a yacht docked near Battery Park City. It seemed like she owned the boat, but she was merely an extravagant house sitter. She had fancy gowns and attended galas and balls. I don't think she owned the gowns, but she got them somehow, and never wore the same thing twice.

It may be unfair to call her a grifter. She's more of a moocher. She never takes money from people; she just uses the things they own but aren't currently using. Imagine you have a penthouse apartment but are rarely in the country. You could hire someone to look after it, to feed your exotic fish, collect your mail, that sort of thing. You might let them occasionally eat dinner there, maybe carry-out from a Chinese place that they wrap up and take with them when they're done. Or, you could let your friend Fiona stay there while you're out of the country. She is going to use all your flatware and the good silver and host big parties almost every night. But don't worry.

When you get back, everything will still be there. She won't have taken anything.

Why would you let her do this? Well, you don't have to pay her, for one thing. Just like Malcolm Lessaker, you're one of those millionaires who's also a tightwad. Maybe you're worried you'll be robbed if the place looks uninhabited. Fiona will definitely make the place look lived-in, and she is conscientious, so nothing will go missing. Plus, you think she is as wealthy as you are. Maybe she gave you a story about just moving back to New York and not having time to find an apartment. "Use mine until you're settled," you tell her. And she does. Part of you thinks she must own some real estate in other exotic locations, and one day she'll return the favor by asking if you want to stay at one of her penthouses. It never crosses your mind that she can't afford a studio apartment, much less a string of luxury suites across the globe. Because when you talk to her, she *seems* rich. She talks like you do. She acts like you do—as if she owns the world and is entitled to it. It's an act, but you haven't met enough poor people to recognize the signs of her humble origins.

The doorman at her current place in SoHo didn't like the looks of me when I announced myself. My suit was obviously not tailored. In fact, it was a sweatsuit. I tried to put on an air of nonchalance like I was a millionaire who had just come from the gym, but he could see through me.

Still, Fiona told him to send me up, so he had no choice.

"Third elevator on the left," he said.

Fiona's place (which wasn't really her place) had its own elevator that didn't stop at the other floors. The walls seemed to be made of actual marble. I stood as non-threateningly as possible while the car ascended, knowing the doorman was watching me on the security camera.

After what seemed like an eternity, the door glided open

silently. There was a small lobby, and Fiona was standing in the open doorway, drinking a glass of champagne.

"Brady!" she said. "Come help me finish this bottle!"

I did.

She also served me a plate of cheese and olives. We lounged in the softest chairs I had ever sat in, so soft that I had trouble relaxing.

"Don't worry, darling, this is not the *good* furniture," she said. "You can sweat on it."

Had I looked like I was sweating? I tried to relax more, although I didn't really feel at ease until the champagne kicked in. We hadn't spoken in a while, so I had forgotten that Fiona always dragged out at least one word in every sentence for emphasis.

"What's up? I haven't seen you in *ages*, Brady! I heard you were working for the man, living the straight life."

"I gave it a go," I said.

"And now here you are! Are you free this weekend? I'm heading out to the Cape with some friends, and you *must* come, you simply must."

"Cape Cod?"

"Oh, you're so funny. I forgot that. Does Cape Cod even *exist* anymore? Do people *go* there? No, no, I hope not. We are going to Cape Canaveral. Some Russian *somebody* rented out the launch pad for a weekend, and we're going to camp out, and that band The Stranger The Fall is playing a set."

"Camping doesn't sound like you."

"*Everyone* goes camping now. I just need to find someone who owns a yurt I can borrow. Small yurts and tiny houses are totally *huge* these days, ever since Gwyneth's personal assistant wrote about them in her zine."

"I don't understand most of what you just said."

"Well, if you can find a tent, I'm sure I can get you a flight down to Florida. Just say the word." She finished her flute of champagne and pranced into the kitchen.

"Tell me *everything* about you since we last saw each other," she called over her shoulder.

I looked around the loft. It was lovely. I have a habit of looking for wires, following where they enter and exit walls, since those are weak points. It's a professional habit, really. Some people would call it *casing a joint*. Those people are mostly cops. There were no visible wires or cords in the loft. Everything floated and hovered, it all looked exquisitely balanced. A television was just flat against the wall. Was the cord embedded in the wall? Was everything wireless? I looked around and saw one of those devices from computer companies that you can talk to if you want it to do something for you. The light switches all had motion detectors. There were small cameras throughout, tastefully hidden amongst the sleek lines of the interior.

Then I saw the apartment through Keisha's eyes and realized it could be recording everything we said. I remembered the story of the Portland family who had a private conversation transcribed and emailed to a co-worker by their Amazon device.

"Is there anywhere else nearby we can go?" I yelled into the kitchen.

"Oh, I know the *perfect* place," Fiona said, coming back into the living room. "It used to be a dive bar in the Meatpacking District and now it's a dive bar-themed cocktail club." She looked at my clothes. "You'll fit in perfectly!"

———

A SHORT WHILE LATER, WE WERE IN THE BACK ROOM OF A luxury clothing store near the Whitney Museum of American Art.

All the way from her loft to the club, she had waved at people she knew, blown air kisses, and seen about seven people she called *darling*.

I was suspicious about my chances of getting into the club. My sweatsuit was a normal, used, plain brown top and bottom that I'd been wearing for years. Anyone in the Meatpacking District who was dressed even remotely like me had designer silk tracksuits, the kind worn by rappers and boy band singers.

But Fiona took care of everything.

First there was a guard outside the club, in black blazer over a black t-shirt.

"Ernest! This is my friend, Mr. Brady Dillinger. We go *way* back, we've known each other *forever*," she said to him. He nodded his head almost imperceptibly. We were in.

Walking through the clothing store at the front of the building, she saluted the staff who were standing around waiting for shoppers, and, I'd guess, slowly starving themselves to death in the quest for ultimate thinness.

She whisked me behind a curtain in the fitting area to a dull gray door that said *Inventory*.

"That's the name of the club: *Inventory*. Cute? Or gross? Comme ci, comme ça."

She pressed a small white button on the wall next to the door and looked up towards a camera a few feet above us to the right.

"Try not to look like a thief," she whispered. I tried.

The door opened and another guard, possibly the identical twin of Ernest from outside, looked us over.

"Big Rich! I didn't know you were back in the city! How *is* your mother?"

"Better," the man said. "She says thank you for the face masks."

He moved aside and we walked towards the bar.

"His mother had foot surgery, so he went back to Atlanta

for a while. I sent her some face masks. The kind for skin care, *not* the kind you wear when you rob a bank."

"I don't wear masks when I rob a bank," I said.

"Of course you don't," she said.

An old oak bar ran the length of the room, but ended abruptly at the wall where the clothing store began, as if some giant had chopped it in half with a cleaver. The wall was polished black marble that worked like a mirror, extending the bar into the distance.

"They wanted to preserve the bar, but they didn't have room for the *whole* thing," Fiona said. "However, they saved the other half and installed it in their Ala Moana shop in Hawaii. And promised to put it back together if they ever vacate this place."

At the bar, a wispy man in a denim shirt with rolled-up sleeves, his arms covered in nautical tattoos, asked what we wanted to drink.

I checked out the row of beer bottles on the wall behind him and asked for a Miller High Life.

"Actually, those are just décor. We don't serve beer," he said. "Cocktails only." He slid me a clipboard with a list of drinks on it. I looked to Fiona for help.

"I'll have a Benson," she said. "He'll have a Meloni. Extra sour. Just like his demeanor." She grabbed my shoulder. "You'll absolutely adore it. Dermot is a *genius*."

She steered me over to a pair of stools in the corner where an old Ms. Pac Man machine served as a table.

"Alright, Mr. Clandestine. Tell me what you're up to this time."

I would say that I told her my plan, but I didn't really have a solid plan at that point. It would be more accurate to say I told her what I was thinking about.

"And you need to know about this Malcolm Lessaker fellow?"

"That's the hope," I said. "I want to know what he's like. First, I want to make sure I haven't made a mistake about him, that he's not secretly donating huge sums of money to charity. Second, just general perceptions of him. Third, any weaknesses. Fourth, any connections to violent crime, the sort of thing that would make this dangerous."

She took a sip of her Benson.

"Do you have a timeline?" she asked.

"I was thinking maybe New Year's."

"Hmm."

"Why do I feel like that's going to be an expensive *Hmm*?" I asked.

"Normally, *dear*, I would wait for a seasonal invite to the District. The Manchesters heading to the Seychelles and leaving their estate open. Or Nestor Piemont-Lewis finally departing the Sandstrom guest cottage. Those sorts of things won't reliably happen until late summer."

"If we don't want to wait?"

"We? I have not agreed to join your *conspiracy* yet."

"Don't use the word conspiracy, please. It's more of a benevolent society."

"*If* time is of the utmost, then I would need to take active measures, setting myself up temporarily at a hotel, to suss out the situation."

"They got Super 8 motels down there?"

She laughed. "I wouldn't know. If we want the wealthy to trust me, they need to think I am one of them. That means, I'm sorry to say, a luxury hotel and some spending money."

"You said *we* just now."

"You know that grammar and consistency have *never* been my strong points." She finished her drink. I was still nursing mine.

"Can you give me a list of some suitable hotels?"

"I would be *delighted*! It's like Christmas morning."

She pranced back to the bar and grabbed a cocktail napkin. From the would-be maritime man, she borrowed a pen, and got a second drink. Then she came back to the table and began writing.

In a few minutes, she handed me the list of hotels. After each one was a number in parentheses.

"Those are my order of preference. Now, it's important that I have a long stay in their system. These kinds of places sometimes get reservations from a one-night *bumpkin*, on a business trip or splurging to see what it's like to be wealthy. To be taken seriously, I need to be booked for at least two weeks. I will, *of course*, try not to stay the duration if I can find other accommodations. But we must be prepared to at least look like we can afford a lengthy visit."

She folded up the napkin and tucked it into the pocket of my sweatsuit.

"This message will self-destruct," she said. "If you accidentally put it in the wash."

"In that case," I said. "I will be sure not to wash this sweatsuit."

"Sometimes I worry about you, Brady."

"What do you think we owe for the drinks?"

"Oh, Clyde is a *friend*, he won't charge us," she said. "Just leave $40 for the tip."

I would have spit out my drink in shock at that point if it hadn't been too expensive to waste a drop.

I left the tip, and it nearly cleaned me out.

TEN

So now I had to find some seed money for Fiona.

There comes a time in any job where you have to decide whether it's really worth it. And that's not just true of robberies. If you're thinking about landscaping your lawn, or building a deck, or making a quilt for your niece, it always starts as an idea. You may look through some home and garden magazines, maybe go to the hardware store and browse through its lumber section, perhaps even buy some knitting supplies and fabric. If you have friends who have taken on similar projects, you'll ask them what they think. You're still just turning over the idea at this point. But once you tear out that big bush you hated near the mailbox, or bury that first big wooden beam, or do whatever the first big part of making a quilt is, well, then, you generally have to finish what you started. Because otherwise that hole or beam or piece of quilt is going to make you feel awful every time you see it.

At this point, I hadn't made a big commitment to the museum job. It was a notion, but I could abandon it. If someone asked me about it later, I could just say, "It didn't quite pan out" and they would understand. There are always some big obstacles, and sometimes you realize, early in the game, that one of them is just insurmountable, or not worth the effort it would take to overcome it.

If you're at the foot of a mountain you want to climb, and a sherpa tells you 75% of people your age die when they try to climb it, you'd be a fool not to turn around and go back where you came from. But if you're 300 feet from the top and your sherpa tells you the same thing, you better climb that last bit because you've come this far, and you're going to climb that mountain even if it kills you. Right?

It doesn't always make sense, but we're humans, and we sometimes do stupid things.

So far, I had only done some poking around into the Lessaker Museum. I hadn't broken any laws, except when I jaywalked a few times on the way to the library to do research. But once I invested some *real* effort, and maybe crossed a legal boundary or two, then I would be in it for the long haul. If some new obstacle arose at that point, I wouldn't just walk away, I'd find a way to beat it.

This was the point when I had to decide whether to really do this thing, whether to cross the Rubicon, as my 11th grade English teacher would have put it. I still did not know whether I could make money off the job, which was an important consideration.

I still needed to talk to Josie, and decided I might as well see her in person. As a bonus, the trip to Vermont and back would give me ample opportunity to collect a petty cash fund for Fiona to get started in Washington.

————

THE NEXT MORNING, I CAUGHT THE 11:33 AM AMTRAK OUT of Penn Station heading north.

There's a few tricks to riding the train for free in the North-east Corridor. First, you need a collection of black markers and one of three types of paper slips the conductor will use to identify passengers. I've got a collection of all of them already. The best way to get them, however, is to follow closely behind a conductor on a train. At some point, they'll stop to engage with an older passenger who has buried their ticket deep in a purse. While the conductor is bent over the passenger's seat, just take a slip or two from their pocket. In a pinch, however, you can usually get by with a small piece of white paper and a small piece of pink paper, because they'll probably use one of those.

At every stop, the conductor checks the tickets of new passengers, and then writes their destination on a small piece of paper which they slot into the railing above the person's seat. Then they don't have to deal with them again until it's time to remind them that their stop is coming up.

So if you don't have a ticket, you walk through the train and find another passenger going to the same stop as you, or a stop that comes after you wish to get off. Note what the conductor has written on their slip of paper and, using the closest marker you have, write the same three-letter code on your slip. In my case, I was going to White River Junction, and I found someone else whose slip said "WRJ." If I was paranoid, I might have tried to find a slip for a later stop like Montpelier or Waterbury and copied that code. That way, if someone asked the conductor about me later, they would probably say I got off at Montpelier or Waterbury. But I know I am nondescript enough to be forgettable when I wish. Often when I don't wish, as well.

The next step is to disperse your things into the seat like you've been on the train for hours. The conductor will be suspicious of anyone who looks like they just got on the train a few moments ago. So I put my bag in the overhead area quickly, then opened my duffle and took out a half-eaten sandwich. I stuck two books in the seat-back pocket in front of me, an almost-empty water bottle on the floor, and an empty candy bar wrapper on the seat next to me. I slipped my forged destination slip into the railing above the seat, folded down the tray table, and put the half-eaten sandwich on it. I looked like I'd been on the train since Philadelphia. A conductor might not remember me, but with all the new passengers boarding simultaneously, they wouldn't stop to ask questions.

Once the train had left the station, but before we got to Stamford, Connecticut, I took a trip to the bathroom and brought my fake WRJ slip with me. I held the rails like I was having trouble walking, and when I got to the seat of the other passenger on the car headed to White River Junction, I slipped my forged stub into the railing above him and took his real one with me. When I got back from the bathroom, I tucked the authentic conductor-made destination slip into the railing above my seat.

As for the other passenger, if a conductor became suspicious of his fake slip, he still had his actual ticket to White River Junction he could provide if questioned.

At least, he did until New Haven, when I distracted him and took it out of his LSAT test prep book, replacing it with a blank piece of paper.

Then for the rest of the trip, I had an authentic ticket in my bag and a genuine destination slip above my seat.

Morally speaking, our government subsidizes highway traffic and car owners far more than it does mass transit users, especially railroad customers. Since I don't own a car, free train trips are my way of balancing out the auto industry and oil company tax subsidies that favor the wealthy and hurt the environment.

Trains are significantly more comfortable than airplanes. You get more leg room. You can get up and walk around without bumping into anyone. Also, they are easier to sneak onto. The drawback, because of that, is that trains are the favored mode of transportation for meth heads, drug dealers, cigarette smokers, sneaks, crooks, and, worst of all, long-winded railroad enthusiasts.

I relaxed for a while as the train took us through Connecticut, and tried to piece together some elements of a plan in my head.

Then I headed for the cafe car, where I had mediocre coffee and a sandwich, and eavesdropped on the other passengers. Many people, myself included, enjoy the comfort of a restaurant booth. So even though the Amtrak seats were more comfortable than an airplane's, passengers congregated in the cafe car to be able to talk and play cards, enjoy the view through the car's bigger windows or the feeling of being nestled between a table and a padded seat. Periodically, the woman behind the counter would remind everyone to share seats, which is how I found myself sitting next to a man who was calling his mistress on the phone.

Based on what I heard from his end of the conversation, she was mad that he wouldn't let her use his secret credit card. He had opened up a new MasterCard in his own name, separate from the ones he shared with his wife. That way he could book hotels for his affairs and buy his mistress gifts without his wife finding out. The card was sent to his business office rather than his home. His mistress wanted to be able to use the card, and to have the bill sent to her house. Maybe she was worried he had multiple mistresses? Maybe she wanted the paperwork to have some power over him? Anyway, the conversation got heated and the man realized he was in a crowded public space.

"Can you watch my stuff for a second?" he asked me, with his hand over the bottom of his phone.

"Sure," I said.

He walked into the passageway between the cars and

began yelling into the phone. The amazing part was that after he stopped yelling, she started yelling back, and we could hear her voice, through the tiny phone, despite the noise of the train and the closed door between us all. Not a fun phone call for him!

He had left his bag on the seat, and I found his wallet, which had a MasterCard tucked deep inside a pocket, away from the other credit cards. And the hidden MasterCard had a first, middle, and last name on it, while his other cards had only his first and last name. So it seemed like that must be the card he used to cover up his affair, and I slipped it into my pocket.

Eventually, he came back into the cafe car, his face flushed red, either from yelling or from the cold of the gangway.

"Women," he said to me. "Sometimes I wonder if they're worth the effort."

I didn't want to make him suspicious of me in case he noticed his missing card anytime soon, but I also didn't want to get into a conversation with him like we were friends.

"No pain, no gain," I said, and shrugged.

"I guess so."

His phone started vibrating and he looked at it.

"Now it's the wife." He sighed.

"I'm going to go back to my seat," I whispered, and he let me out of the booth as he answered his phone in a too-pleasant voice.

———

THE TRAIN RAN THROUGH THE FOREST, SOMETIMES ALONG THE water. In New England, having switched from electric to diesel, the track ran much closer to trees and water, without the need for unsightly towers and cables parallel to the track. The hypnotic procession of pine trees lulled me into a trance from which I considered the situation at hand. I could not come up with any new conclusions, so I pulled out the railroad magazine from the seat back in front of me. A country musician was on the cover. Inside, apart from the profile of the singer, there were a few short descriptions of cities served by train and activities to enjoy in each one. Nothing terribly interesting to me. Other than Clyde, who didn't actually read them, I only knew one person who subscribed to magazines about railroads, and his last name was Vanderbilt.

Then there was a pull-out section advertising a train you could load your car on to travel from Virginia to Florida. I did not own a car, but I was curious why you would put your car on a train instead of driving the car. Could you put a bicycle inside your car inside the train? How many different modes of transportation could you nest inside each other on the one train?

I looked at a section about Washington, D.C., to see if it had any helpful information, since it was near the Lessaker Museum. There was a list of new musicals opening in town. And then a short blurb about the city's seafood markets. Perhaps stolen paintings could be stuffed inside fresh fish to conceal them? Probably not, the smell would be unbearable.

Soon I had read the whole short magazine.

It's important to remember to bring books when traveling. Luckily, I had the two books with me that I had used as props to make it look like I had been on the train longer than I had.

The first was a history of five women artists in New York in the second half of the twentieth century. It seemed like a good idea to bone up on some art knowledge in case I found myself having to pretend to be someone passionate about art. Plus, I like any book about New York City.

The other book was a guide to investing for young people. I was not young, and did not have any money to invest, but hoped to one day acquire both youth and wealth.

The time passed, and soon we had arrived at White River Junction, which is a classic small town with a train track running through the middle of it, across from Main Street. I repacked all my belongings into my duffel and hopped off at the station, along with several older people, some young college students, and the LSAT-studying man. Many of them had cars waiting for them. I waited until the train had pulled out of town, and crossed the tracks to the big brick Hotel Coolidge that occupied a whole block of the town's main thoroughfare.

Inside, it was like time had stopped passing sometime in the 1950s. Not in a Miss Havisham sort of way—there was WiFi, and it was clean. But the architecture preserved all the wood ornamentation of the original building. The front desk seemed to be where it had presumably always been. The hotel had managed to escape the soulless renovation that plagued these sorts of buildings in the 1980s and 1990s. No tile floor or poured-cement industrial aesthetic here. It was all carpets, wood, and chandeliers. I got a room for under $100, paid in cash, and took my things up the stairs to 216.

After washing my face in the bathroom sink, I left the hotel and walked out of town, past the local car dealer and then the church, up a small hill to Josie's place. I could have tried calling again, but it seemed in the spirit of rural New England neigh-borliness to just show up and ring the doorbell. Her house was a small split level ranch with a big shed in the back. When no one answered the door, I walked around to the rear of the house to see if she was doing yard work, or hanging clothes on a laundry line, or making moonshine. I wasn't really sure what people did to pass time out here in the country.

She wasn't in the backyard, so I opened the door of the shed, which had been converted into an art studio. Josie wasn't in there painting, so I poked around and looked at some of her canvases. Most were pictures of people with masks on. Cheap halloween masks, generally, but a few were wearing fancy masquerade costumes. I picked up one of a woman with a red handkerchief tied around her face like a Wild West bank robber.

"So it's true, Brady? You've become an art thief once again?"

ELEVEN

THE VOICE SEEMED TO COME FROM ALL AROUND ME.

I looked up and saw two speakers nailed into the rafters of the shed.

"That one's not for sale," Josie's voice said, and I put the painting down. "I'm in the main house. I'll come back there and meet you."

I turned and looked out the door of the art studio, then saw her pull open the house's sliding glass door and walk towards me. Josie was very tall, and wore clothing that, I would say, did not look like normal clothing. This time she was draped beneath a knee-length red sleeveless sweater. Her glasses seemed to be connected by a gold chain to a necklace that looked like it had melted onto her chest. She walked along the path to the shed and made a *tsk-tsk-tsk* sound as she got closer. I should mention that we used to date, a long time ago.

"Caught in the act, it seems," she said.

"I was just admiring your work. This one is really nice." I pointed to grid filled with dots near the door

"Ah, yes, I copied that from a dead woman. It was a tragedy, she died so young. Thus, she was not around to capitalize on the fame she acquired after death, and I thought I would help remedy the situation by putting more of her work into the world."

She walked over and picked up the painting.

"Did you see the documentary they made about her?"

"Probably not," I answered.

"I can summarize it. The art world treats women horribly. Men take credit for their work or steal their ideas. They die young or internalize the unfairness and go crazy. When women go crazy, they get locked away. Men who go crazy are celebrated for it."

"Sad," I said. "What's that a picture of, anyway?"

"Oh, dear. It's cute that you think people still paint pictures *of* things." She put the canvas down. "I am famished. I was about to go get dinner. Would you care to join me?"

"Yes, please. By the way, did you get my messages? You never called me back."

"I tried, but there was a problem with the number, it was a ramen restaurant in SoHo. For a while I thought you had retired and gone into the food business."

She handed me her cell phone and showed the number she had called on the screen. The last two digits were 2-6 instead of 3-3.

"You were supposed to dial Larry Bird's jersey number at the end," I said.

"I don't know who that is. I asked one of my students what number Bird from the Celtics wore in basketball and they told me 26."

She looked something up on her phone's internet for a moment. "Oh, I guess that's a man named Jabari Bird, not Larry Bird. Anyway, if you're ever hungry for ramen, you can call this number."

She locked the door of the shed behind us, and we walked towards the street that led into town.

"Don't you need to lock the house too?"

"I leave that open. It's a New England thing. But now that there's a thief in town, I feel compelled to worry about the security of my studio." Here, she winked at me.

The sky was starting to display the first hints of night as we strolled down South Main Street.

"There's a barbecue place up near the train tracks," she said, pointing to our destination.

"Can you eat barbecue in that sweater?"

"I can eat barbecue in anything, Brady."

I paid with the credit card from the cheater on the train, and we sat out on the restaurant's porch, enjoying pulled pork sandwiches and the brisk air of the coming night. A group of friends was sitting at a table nearby, so we caught up on our personal lives to make sure they wouldn't overhear us discussing anything illegal. I told her about my job at the air conditioning school, and she told me about a dying stock-broker who proposed to her in Switzerland the previous summer.

"I told him no, of course," she said. "Not because he was dying, but because he was a stockbroker. In any event, I believe I have lived alone too long to be able to enter a marriage at this point." She did not seem unhappy as she said this.

Finally, the other party on the porch left, a waiter cleared our trays and brought me a beer and Josie a wine. We got down to business.

I described the Lessaker Museum, and she said she was familiar with it.

"They are notorious for not loaning out their works," she said. "Art hoarders."

I explained that I was unsure about the prospects of unloading stolen art, especially in such large quantities, from a well-known source.

"In the past, one or twice, I've come into possession of an

artwork or two, and you helped me find a buyer, but those times were usually by accident."

"I remember."

"But knocking off a whole museum," I said. "I don't really know if it can be profitable. I'm wondering if there's an angle I don't know about, maybe you could help me with."

She sipped at her wine and thought for a while.

"The obvious answer is not a good one. You could sell to the Russians and Chinese."

"Communists like art that much?"

She laughed.

"The Russians aren't communist anymore, Brady. Nor the Chinese either, really. But both countries have millionaires and repressive regimes. A ruthless person can build a fortune in those places, but it is almost impossible to get that fortune out of the country since the leaders do not want their rubles and yuan waltzing off to America and becoming dollars."

"Tough to be an international gangster these days," I said.

"They can just throw you in jail over there, or worse, you have an accident and fall off a building. It motivates people to stay in the country. But the upshot of it is that they're constantly looking for ways to smuggle out their money. Enter the art market.

"Dictators do not keep a close watch on the art world. They appreciate when works by big names enter the country, because that makes the nation look good. So gangsters use galleries and auctions to help get their money into America. In one transaction, they'll overpay for a work that ends up in China, and then underpay for a work that stays in America. Eventually, when they resell the work in America, the extra money stays in a U.S. bank account for them to access later.

"And there's the black market for stolen art, of course. Paintings are easier to smuggle across a border than large stacks of cash or gold, which is obviously quite heavy. You know, in China, they have these little factories where peasants churn out forgeries of Picassos and Monets, painted by hand. It's not hard to slip a real Picasso into the stack, and nobody blinks since the actual item looks so much like the rest of counterfeit works. So that's another vehicle for sneaking fortunes out of the country.

"There are two big drawbacks. The first is that you would be dealing with gangsters and criminals. The second is that they only deal in big names. Because the art is a proxy for cash, they stick with reliable heavy hitters. Not to mention, they tend to be sexist. But the Lessaker Museum generally traffics in more conceptual art and a fair amount of women. Try telling Viktor from Moscow that you want him to invest in a Louise Bourgeois watercolor. *Nyet!* Sorry. It would be hard to break even on a museum job like that, much less make it profitable enough to risk the jail time."

"Bummer," I said.

We sat in the darkness for a while.

"There is one other thing," she said.

I smiled. Jose always came through.

"There are rumors that Lessaker has been dipping his toes into the black market. Inquiring about off-the-books sales."

"Buying or selling?"

"Buying, generally. The word on the boulevard is that Lessaker is moving his fortune out of the reach of IRS accountants and the government. Lately, he has been making large charitable gifts to some less reputable organizations. Some people think those are cover transactions for him buying stolen art and antiquities."

"The more I learn about this guy, the less I like him."

"I should warn you that it's idle chatter. As my students would say, just *hot goss* at this point. He may just be reaching the end of his life and trying to spread his largesse around."

She laughed, and then I did. Neither of us believed he might have suddenly grown generous.

"But if he's not donating to legit charities, he must be up to something," I said.

"Again, it's speculation, but the tide has been turning against opioid manufacturers. Purdue and the Sacklers just agreed to pay Oklahoma $270 million to avoid a trial. And that's only one state out of 50."

"Lessaker is essentially a heroin dealer."

"Indeed. So the theory is that he's eliminating his wealth on paper to protect himself from future lawsuits, but making sure he can still access his fortune down the road."

"Like a drug dealer stashing a bunch of money with his mistress before going to prison?"

"I suppose. Except that in this case, stolen art is his mistress."

The staff of the restaurant hinted that it was closing time, so we made our way back towards town.

"The museum on campus just reopened," she said. "If you want to take a look around tomorrow. Plus they have a lot of conceptual art on view. They rehung and put a lot of the old white men's paintings into storage."

"So you're saying it's mostly weird shit now?"

"Ah, but it's *good* weird shit. And similar to what Lessaker has in his collection. Just promise not to steal anything."

"I would never steal from a friend."

We got to the front of my hotel and said goodbye. I went up to my room and read a few chapters of the book about women artists. To be honest, I skimmed a lot of it and mostly looked at the pictures.

TWELVE

THE NEXT MORNING, I TOOK A FREE PUBLIC BUS ACROSS THE
river to the college in New Hampshire where Josie worked. It
was the type of scenic ivy-covered school where you imagined
a guy named Chip would turn up in his thick, white sweater at
any minute to invite you on a weekend ski trip. Muffy would be
in the car next to him already. You would probably decline
because you already had plans to sail around Portsmouth on
Dougie Flynn's yacht.

I found a brochure for a self-guided walking tour of all the
public art on campus and started with that. The trick to faking
your way through any field of knowledge is to learn the basic
stuff everyone knows, and then have a few esoteric pieces of
knowledge to sprinkle on top, like icing on the cake, if icing
could be sprinkled. Being familiar with some random sculptures in New Hampshire seemed like a good ruse to have up
my sleeve in case I fell into any art conversations during the
next few months of heist planning.

Over the next hour, I saw a couple of big hunks of metal, a
long white wooden triangle that looked like an airplane had
crashed into the lawn, a big iron and wood scale that didn't

weigh anything, a lifelike sculpture of Robert Frost sitting on a bench, a stack of rocks, and five giant rectangles hanging from a building that had been painted primary colors. I would have to ask Josie later what they all meant.

Walking by the library, I saw a flyer tacked to a bulletin board advertising a fraternity party that night to raise money for the house's legal fund. Inside the library, I used one of the free computer kiosks to look up the fraternity in the campus newspaper. Apparently, the college was trying to remove them from campus for repeated violations of sexual harassment and assault rules. They needed to pay lawyers who would sue to keep them from getting kicked off. According to the flyer, various historical items from the fraternity's illustrious history could be purchased later that day, along with "cool $5 shots." While I did not wish to buy anything they were selling, I noted that the auction ran until 8:00 PM, which was after the banks would have closed. This told me that the fraternity would not be able to deposit any funds they raised until the next morning. It seemed dangerous to keep all that money in a house full of drunk people in a part of New England where everyone left their doors unlocked all the time. Especially with a practiced thief wandering around campus.

———

I MADE MY WAY ACROSS A BIG GREEN LAWN TO THE HOOD Museum, which was free to enter, like all museums should be. I noted the configurations of the cameras and various other monitors. I wasn't planning to steal anything, but Josie had told me the place just reopened, so I figured the security would be state-of-the art and worth learning about.

I made a few sketches on a small pad of paper from the hotel. There were multiple sensors, some probably for temperature and humidity. I wondered if they were connected to the same communication lines as the cameras.

It was a small enough museum that it probably did not have a room full of TV monitors constantly watched by multiple people. Maybe there was one person in such a room, but most likely the cameras were there to record what happened in case someone needed to check the footage later. I doubted there were multiple overnight guards doing rounds, certainly not former cops or other large people. If they had a surplus of security, it was related to the college's need to employ students in exchange for federal funding. So, young kids rather than well-trained guards. As it was located right in the middle of campus, there were pedestrians passing by at all hours, and it would be hard to sneak away with an armload of art without somebody noticing.

The Lessaker Museum, on the other hand, was nestled in the woods and had no cache of student labor to pull from. From what I knew of Lessaker's greediness, he would spend as little as possible on security, so it would probably not be guarded too heavily at night. As Josie had said, there was little profit in robbing a building full of conceptual art, so Lessaker was unlikely to spend much money guarding against the possibility.

Continuing my journey through the Hood Museum, I soon found myself in front of a large painting of a gas station at night. It was over 10 feet long and five feet high. It was beautiful, and I thought that if I was going to steal anything from this museum, this would be it. So I ran through the logistics, just as mental exercise. The painting would be nearly impossible to get out of the museum in its frame. That would take at least two men, or women, and be very obvious. Taking it off the frame and rolling it would be an option, but that seemed likely to create creases and cracks in the stark black triangle of night that made up half the canvas. I was stumped. It became clear that, beyond the difficulties of making a profit from oversized works on the stolen art market, there was a purely logistical reason why art thieves of the past had focused on smaller works and portraits. The largest painting stolen from the Gardner Museum in Boston was half the size of the gas station I stood in front of; the rest were significantly smaller.

I found my way to a different gallery filled with historical artifacts. Lining the walls were giant stone Assyrian reliefs from 800 BC. According to the brochure, they were donated to the collection by a British colonialist named Rawlinson, who worked for the British East India Company. I have to admit, those guys in the 1800s really knew how to steal art: Show up with an army, chisel everything off the walls, pack it up into crates, and ship it all back home. They did it all in broad daylight, too. Yet instead of being arrested, they were applauded—Rawlinson received an honorary degree from the college for donating all the art he looted from a palace in Iraq, art that had never belonged to him in the first place.

The pieces themselves were inspiring. While the scale was massive, the details remained intricate, and they managed to convey great depth despite only an inch or so of thickness. You could see the weave of the robes the men wore, the strands of hair in their beards. I suppose the sculptures had originally been built into whatever location had been their original home, but here they were given geometric symmetry, framed like individual works of art, and I could see why someone, despite the horrible act of cultural desecration, would want to steal them.

Standing there, I had an epiphany.

I realized I could rob the Lessaker Museum the same way the British had plundered the Near East in the 19th Century—not in darkness, but in plain sight.

I finished up in the museum and wandered around the small New Hampshire town the rest of the afternoon, before getting dinner at an Indian restaurant.

Later that night, someone robbed the fraternity I had read about and made off with over ten thousand dollars.

From what I heard, the thief got away with exactly $11,120. He also took a supply of illegal date-rape drugs that he had found hidden near the cash, although that part was never reported in the media. Nobody saw the guy, but I have a very strong suspicion that he looked exactly like me.

THIRTEEN

BACK IN NEW YORK, I GOT IN TOUCH WITH FIONA, AND GAVE her some spending money. She decamped for Washington, D.C., where I would contact her with more details later. In the meantime, she bounced her way into high society there and inched her way towards the Lessaker family.

Next, I got in touch with Clyde and Keisha. I updated them on my thinking, and Keisha told me what she had been able to uncover so far. It was not a lot, but she was still finishing her degree and said she'd have more free time in the summer. She asked me to try to get us on a tour of the Lessaker Museum so that she could assess their systems in person, maybe even scope out their wireless set-up. I explained that they very rarely gave tours because it wasn't a real museum, but I'd see what I could do.

We had reached the point of no return.

I began looking into how art is transported and stored under normal conditions. I stalked some art galleries and museums and followed employees to local bars on Thursdays and Fridays. Then I started up random conversations with them, playing myself off as some weird loner who just liked chatting with strangers. This may have been the hardest part of the whole caper, as I do not like talking to people I don't know. I can barely stand talking to people I *do* know. Still, I asked them what they did, then followed up with specific questions I wanted answered, mixed in with some irrelevant questions too, so they wouldn't remember me as the guy who just asked about art shipping and security.

For instance, I'd ask whether there were any electronic markers inside a crate with a painting, then I'd follow up by asking if there was a law about how many colors a painter could use on one painting. Then a little later, I'd ask how thorough a condition check was when art was uncrated, after which I'd ask if painters ever hid treasure maps in their paintings "like that guy Salvador Dalivinci did." I seemed like a harmless fool.

At each bar, I described my occupation differently so that they would never connect the conversations back to the real me later. Once I claimed I was a pickle briner; another time I said I ran a daycare center for rich kids' dolls. My favorite fake job was helicopter safety inspector for the FAA. "You'd be surprised," I told them, "how often a helicopter tries to take off without enough blades. Too many companies cut corners on maintenance that way."

After a few weeks, I had all the information I needed, which was good, because these people hated their jobs and spent *a lot* of money at the bar, making it hard for me to keep up with their drinking.

———

NEXT, I HAD TO GET MYSELF INTO A TOUR GROUP TO SEE THE Lessaker Museum in person. This would be difficult, as I told Keisha, because they only gave tours several times a year, since it was not really a museum, except for tax purposes.

Byron Soop might have been able to get me in with his connection to the place from when he installed its air conditioning system, but then my visit would be traceable back to me through him. I needed to go undercover, so there would be nothing linking me to the museum I planned to rob.

The best option seemed to be pretending I was an art student writing a thesis on one of the artists they were exhibiting. I looked up what would be on display during their next tour period and decided to claim I was studying the works of Mayslie Retepps, a woman who had worked with discarded curtain fabric and died tragically young. Her dying young was great for my purposes, because it meant she had only a small body of work that I had to familiarize myself with, although it was obviously a bit of a bummer for her.

I met up with Keisha at a cafe downtown, near NYU, the kind of place where students and freelancers buy one coffee in the morning and then spread themselves out over two chairs and work for several hours. I needed her help submitting a request for one of the tour slots. She had already done most of the work.

"First," she said, "I set up a fake email that looks like it comes from a faculty member of The Institute of Fine Arts." She handed me a slip of paper with an email address that looked like an actual professor's account. Underneath it was another email address and password. "The fake one will forward to that account. If they follow up for a recommendation or to verify, it will show up in the second account. At that point, you can write a response from the professor, and I'll send it so that it looks like it came from that fancy college email address."

Next we went over my application essay, and then she "bounced us off an NYU server" to submit the whole package "through an IP that looked like theirs." I had no idea what that meant, but Keisha said it was called *spoofing*.

"I doubt they're keeping track of where these applications come from," she said. "But just in case they're logging them, if they look back later to find any suspicious behavior, this will just seem like a real submission from an NYU student." She finished her coffee and began eating a scone.

I asked her if she wanted to submit an application too, so that she could get a sense of their electronic security system.

"We shouldn't go together, obviously, but we can submit another application for you," I said.

She smiled.

"I already have an appointment to take a tour next week, under the name of Sara Cusmar-Burns. She will be there on behalf of a feminist art collective from Brooklyn. The museum is hosting a special tour group for women, led by *Mrs. Malcom Lessaker* herself. My coursework this semester was easier than I thought, so I didn't have to wait until summer."

"You're a quick study on this sort of thing."

"Which reminds me, I need to stop by a thrift store and buy some ridiculous clothes so that I can pass for an artist."

"It's also a benefit if people remember your weird clothes more than they remember you."

"That's what Clyde told me, too. I'm thinking about some fake piercings as well."

"We should probably avoid the thrift stores in the city," I said. "A lot of times, they're pricier than the stores that sell new clothes."

"That's because people prefer stuff that's old and has already stood the test of time. With new stuff, you're always taking a chance."

———

A FEW WEEKS LATER, I MET UP WITH FIONA AT AN ETHIOPIAN restaurant in Washington.

"No offense, Brady, but I *can't* be seen with you at any of my usual haunts."

"I get it, I'm a known criminal."

"It's not that, *dear*, it's your clothing."

I was wearing a sweaty tracksuit again, although it wasn't the one I'd worn before.

"I have a *reputation* to maintain, you know. Anyway, look at these pictures before the food comes. We'll be eating with our fingers here, and it will make a mess of my screen."

She handed me her phone, and I scrolled through her photos. They were mostly selfies and she was making the same duck face in all of them. They weren't very good, and I told her so after looking at a few and putting the phone down. "But don't take it personal, I'm not much of a selfie enthusiast."

"Darling, you are as thick as porridge sometimes. I know how to take a good selfie when I want to. These are *intentionally* bad. I took them at the Lessaker Mansion."

I scrolled back to the beginning and had another look. They *were* bad, I had that part right. In many of them, her face was out of focus and not centered.

"It wasn't easy to do, I might add," Fiona said. "These bloody phones work so hard to focus on the human face, it can be a real *bear* getting them to focus on something else."

Then I noticed what she was talking about in one of her photos. While she was making her stupid selfie face, she had actually focused her phone's camera on the wall behind her. Along the crown molding, there was a small white device that seemed like it might be a camera.

"I am not sure that those are all for security purposes," she said. "They also have wireless speakers and those talking computer gizmos *everywhere*, but I photographed everything just to be safe."

I kept scrolling, and noted some sort of device in every picture until I came to the end. Then she reached across the table and handed me a small hand-drawn map of the mansion. It was on Lessaker Foundation stationary.

"I found *tons* of it in a drawer in his wife's office," she said.

The map had numbers written all over it.

"The numbers correspond to the photos, so you know where each was taken."

"Well, this is impressive," I said. "If I decide to rob the Lessaker Mansion, it will be useful."

"Ah, yes, you would prefer to have *this*, I suppose." She handed me another hand-drawn map. This one was of the Lessaker Museum. "After a few hours of cocktails, they took us on a private tour of their *collection*. We walked through the galleries, but they also showed us their storage space."

The map was nice, but photos would have been better.

"I thought it might be a tad suspicious for me to take *oodles* of pictures in the museum itself, so I did not get any." She frowned. And then she reached into her handbag and pulled out another iPhone. "But *Gloryia* took a whole bunch."

"Who is Gloryia? Isn't she going to miss her phone? Or report it stolen and wipe its memory?"

"Gloryia is an aspiring *Real Housewife* who was *also* at the Lessaker Mansion with me. She had *too much* to drink and lost her phone. Well, to be honest, *I* distracted her and took it. She thinks one of the limo drivers found it in his car later and is going to bring it to her place this weekend. She had wanted an upgrade anyway, so she bought a *new* phone in the meantime, which means she's in no rush to get this back."

I pondered this for a bit but was still confused.

"Your forehead is getting *scrunched*, Brady. Let me explain. Keisha helped me set up an email account for one of the drivers, and then the *fake* driver contacted Gloryia to let her know he had found her phone. That way she stopped worrying about it."

"I still don't know who Gloryia is."

"She is *nobody*, dear. Would you like to see the photos?"

"Uh, sure."

Fiona turned the phone on.

"Don't you need her passcode or fingerprint or face recognition or something?"

"Rich people seldom bother with that, since they *never* go places where they think someone might steal their phone. They are surrounded by the wealthy all the time. So," she wagged the phone at me, "they become *entirely* too trusting."

She brought up the photo gallery, and I skimmed through the photos taken inside the Lessaker Museum.

"Can I email these to myself?"

"Darling, no! The sent messages would show up in her email account. But fear not, Keisha has downloaded them onto a hard drive."

"Oh, good."

Our food arrived and we put away everything on the table and began eating.

"If Keisha already has the photos, why did you need to show me the phone?"

"For the dramatic *reveal*, Brady. And by the way, we need someone to pretend to be the driver and return her phone this weekend."

That turned out to be me.

FOURTEEN

"CONGRATULATIONS! YOU HAVE BEEN SELECTED FOR A TOUR OF
the Lessaker Museum," the letter said. "Please read below for
further instructions about your upcoming visit. Be advised that
we cannot change or reschedule appointments, and visitors
who cancel or do not show up will not be allowed to visit the
Lessaker Museum again for a minimum of three (3) years.
Formal dress is required. Photography is not allowed. This invi-
tation may not be transferred and has no cash value…"

Finally, I would get the opportunity to see the place I was
going to rob. By now, Fiona and Keisha had already seen it
before me, and I was starting to feel like a third wheel on this
caper.

The letter was actually just an email sent to the account
Keisha had set up for me. You might think that a big expensive
foundation would send out invitations on glossy card stock, but
you would have overestimated the stinginess of this particular
subset of the elite.

I had just a few weeks to get ready for my visit. First, I
needed formal attire, so I went to the Brooks Brothers store at
the Tyson's Corner Center mall and had a blue pinstripe suit

tailored to fit me. For an extra fee, they were able to have it ready in just two days. Sadly, after the suit was finished but before I paid for it, the store was robbed by a man dressed as a maintenance worker. The thief, who looked very much like me, made off with several custom suits from their storage room, as well as a number of dress shirts which were later donated to a charity that helps disadvantaged D.C. residents find appropriate clothing for job interviews and employment.

After that, I needed cameras that I could sneak past security at the Lessaker Museum, so I went to the gift shop of the Spy Museum to grab some free gear. For a place dedicated to espionage and intrigue, they had very little in-store security. A man with my thieving experience could—and did—walk away with a lot of their inventory.

Then I needed a haircut that made me look like someone interested in art. It was a bit of a risk—on the one hand, getting a haircut that was a little flashy would draw extra attention to me. On the other hand, showing up as a middle aged man with a normal haircut posing as a graduate student in contemporary art would seem even weirder. I decided that having people focus on my strange haircut would take their attention away from my face, which was a plus, since I would change my hair again after the museum trip.

Keisha suggested the possibility of something called dazzle camouflage, which had been used during World War II to disguise the size and shapes of battleships and other boats, using angular stripes and geometric shapes that confused the eye. Apparently, a version of it could be applied to one's hair and face to confuse modern facial recognition software so that it did not even register you as a human with a face. Although that sounded fun, when I saw what it looked like, I didn't think I could get away with wearing it in public at my age. So I opted to have my hair dyed a variety of bright colors, pink and green, and fleshed out the look with some fake piercings on my ears.

To round out my aesthetic, I needed some interesting glasses—what Fiona termed "architect glasses." Apparently, all the big-name building designers wear weird spectacles. On top of that, the right lenses could also help distort my appearance on any cameras that picked me up. This meant I had to also get prescription contacts to cancel out the effects of the glass lenses so I could still see and not develop an incapacitating headache during the museum tour.

Altogether, I did not look like myself. I assembled the whole costume in the pool house of the place where Fiona was now staying, having checked out of her hotel to house-sit a mansion on the same wealthy street where boxer Sugar Ray Leonard had once lived. Fiona and Kiesha were both sitting by the pool drinking rosé when I walked out like a runway model in my new suit, haircut, and glasses.

I stopped far away from them because my peripheral vision was distorted by the combination of contacts and glasses. I felt like I could fall into the pool at any step.

"Come *closer*, darling!"

"Yeah," Keisha said, "don't be shy."

I walked deliberately, slowly lifting one foot and putting it down in front of me, and then doing the same with the next. "I think my eyes will adjust in a bit."

"If they don't, you're out of luck," Keisha said. "For all the effort you put into the disguise, everyone is going to remember very clearly a guy who walks like that."

"You look like an *astronaut* in training, Brady. Are you practicing for a moon landing?"

With each step, my brain adjusted a bit, and I grew more confident. I practically danced the last three steps toward them.

"*There* it is! Now do a spin and let us watch you walk away."

"I feel objectified."

Fiona whistled like she was on a fox hunt.

"The question is, would you be able to recall my face later?"

"No, just that sweet ass!" Keisha said.

They both laughed at me.

———

NEXT, I NEEDED A CAR.

Anyone can steal a car—teenagers do it all the time. The real trick is getting away with the vehicle intact, being able to keep the car instead of ditching it after a joy ride or dumping it at a chop shop.

The best method is to take a car that nobody will miss. This doesn't necessarily mean a cheap car seemingly forgotten at the side of the road. Sometimes those old junkers cause the biggest problems, because their owners are so poor that, surprising as it may be, the run-down, rusted shell of an automobile is their most prized possession.

On the other hand, there are limousine companies sitting on extra dozens of big SUVs. And mid-life crisis corporate lawyers often have spare garages full of tarp-covered classic convertibles. The nice thing about those situations is that you just need to prop up the tarp with something shaped like the car and a casual glance will fail to notice the vehicle's absence. But I did not want a flashy old convertible for this trip; I needed something bland and unmemorable.

A private security company which had changed names several times as a result of disastrous adventures in some recent wars had a logistics headquarters in northern Virginia. In addition to exporting American misdeeds and ill will to small countries unfortunate enough to be sitting on top of big oil deposits, the company sometimes provided security in the U.S., roughing up environmental protestors or protecting visiting dictators.

For these tasks, they had a fleet of oversized black sedans

and SUVs with tinted windows stored behind a chain-link fence with barbed wire spooled out along the top. Although it looked intimidating and ruined the neighborhood it was in, it was surprisingly easy to bypass considering that the company claimed to specialize in protecting assets. While they might notice the missing car, since I did very little to hide its absence, I doubted they had the competence to track it down. They were good at making a big show of force and intimidating people, but brains were not their strongpoint.

While I was in the parking lot liberating a luxury SUV, I deflated some tires and disconnected a bunch of other vehicles' tail lights, so that future tyrants visiting from problematic countries would get pulled over while being chauffeured around the nation's capital by this company. I considered it a public service.

———

THE APPOINTED DAY CAME. I DONNED MY OUTFIT AND HOPPED in the back of the car, which was being driven by some guy I hired from a local improv theater. Fiona and Keisha could not do it, because they had already been to the Lessaker Museum, and they might be recognized, not to mention the fact that most rich people would frown upon the idea of having a woman as a chauffeur, because their attitudes are still firmly embedded in the 19th Century.

I hadn't gotten a uniform for my driver, so I just asked him to wear a nice shirt and pants, and he said that was what he wore at all his improv shows anyway, and then he tried really hard to get me to go to one sometime. I told him my doctor had diagnosed me with high blood pressure and it would be unhealthy for me to watch someone embarrass themselves, which meant I could not attend an improv comedy show.

He typed the museum's address into his phone, but the neighborhood was not visible on the map.

"Oh, I've seen this before," he said. "Kim and Kanye had their neighborhood taken off the grid, too. It's something rich people can do."

"Have you worked as a chauffeur in the past?"

"Not in real life, but I often pretend to drive limousines in my shows. For instance, last week, we did a scene set in Paris—"

I cut him off and read him the directions that had been emailed to me from the Lessaker Foundation. He started driving.

We were on our way.

FIFTEEN

WE TOOK A CIRCUITOUS ROUTE, THROUGH THE SHADY
esplanades of the elite, the bucolic pastures of success, and the
hidden acres of the deceitful. Every house we passed was
unique in its own vulgar fashion. As much as people dislike the
cookie-cutter suburbs with their matching, mass-produced two-
garage homes, this was far worse. The whims of every fortune
were on display with no cohesion at all.

Some houses were not just at odds with the house next
door but with themselves, built by one millionaire in a specific
style thirty years ago, then sold to a multi-millionaire with
different tastes in the past decade, forcing a conversion from,
say, colonial manor, to a pastiche of mid-century modern. The
jangled and monstrous results were like the pulled and prodded
faces of the rich who lived inside—the bones beneath no
longer bearing any relation to the surface features. In the case
of the mansions, various zoning restrictions prohibited the
wholesale destruction of an old home and fresh start; in a
similar fashion, prenuptial agreements prevented many wealthy
old men and women from getting rid of their aging spouse in
favor of something new and fresh. The solution, in marriages,

was to arrange for a young lover on the side. When it came to estates, you could often find a recently built guest house in a more modern style encroaching on the aging, original home.

The Lessaker land was a prime example of this. We pulled in through wrought iron gates attached to stately brick columns that matched the palatial facade of their home, which should have been a grand manor. But undercutting the impression was a glimpse in the distance of the sleek lines of the museum, the polished white stone and glass, lithe and delicate, which suddenly made the red brick fortress of a house seem clumsy and ridiculous, like an oaf of a bodybuilder being beaten up by a small, thin martial arts expert.

The gate we had passed through remained open, I noticed. I guessed they were just going to leave it open all day as the scheduled visitors arrived. Already, the driveway was filled with cars, though it was big enough not to be crowded. The perimeter fencing was easily climbable, but getting a vehicle in and out for a heist would require opening the gate, unless the museum had a service entrance I hadn't yet seen.

I got out of the car and joined a group of people milling about near the despicably ugly fountain in the middle of the driveway. Most of the men and women seemed like standard corporate titans, weathered trophy wives, and overly educated, pipe-smoking descendants of Gilded Age fortunes. Hopefully I fit in with that last group, visually, as if I was someone who never needed a job and hopped around from one degree to another.

But there was one woman who did not fit in with the others. She was younger, for one thing, and certainly less stiff. While everyone else stood, she sat on the edge of the fountain with her knees pulled up under her chin. She had the same haircut they gave out for free at basic training in the army, shaved down to just a blond fuzz around the shape of her skull.

I made eye contact with her, and she spit in the fountain while staring at me.

A man with a radio handset approached her.

"Excuse me, ma'am, they would rather you not leave your bicycle in the driveway."

"Who are they?" she asked.

"I'm not sure I understand," he said.

"The Lessakers don't want my bike in their driveway?"

"No, I don't speak directly with them. I talked to the head of security."

"It's a security risk to have a bike in the driveway?"

"He's in charge of security *and* grounds and appearances."

"So he doesn't want my bike to appear on the grounds?"

"Let's not make this a big deal, ma'am."

"Stop calling me that. Just to be clear, you're saying the Lessaker Museum doesn't allow guests to use environmentally friendly modes of transportation like bicycles and would prefer patrons arrive by car?"

"Give me one second, ma'am … or … um, miss."

"That's also bad, don't assign me a gender and condescend to me at the same time."

He stepped away and spoke into the radio for a bit out of earshot. I headed over towards the fountain.

"Aren't you worried they won't let you in if you cause too many problems?" I asked.

"Eh, their collection's not that good, and besides it will look worse for them if they keep me out. I'm writing the place up for *The Hypochondriac.*"

"Is that a magazine for people who think they're sick?"

"No, it's an influential art world publication."

"Why's it called *The Hypochondriac*?"

"I don't know, I wasn't there when it started. They probably thought it was funny at the time. Plus, it's journal of contemporary art, it's not supposed to make sense." She looked me up and down slowly. "Midlife crisis?"

"What? No. I'm not." I coughed. "Having a midlife crisis, I mean. Why do you ask?"

"I can tell that's a recent hair cut from the tan lines on your head. Plus you're wearing new glasses and clothes. And you don't seem to know much about the art world, so I'm guessing that it's a recent interest of yours. To top it all off, you ignored the other people your age and came to talk to the woman who is young enough to be your daughter. Seems like a pretty standard midlife crisis."

I was coming up with a particularly cutting and funny retort when the security guard came back and interrupted us.

"They say you can leave your bicycle in the garage, if that is agreeable with you."

"The Lessakers' garage, right? Not the servants' one."

"Um, excuse me for one more second," he said and stepped away again.

I reached out my hand to introduce myself to the woman. "I'm, uh, …" I temporarily forgot the name I had used to register for the tour. "Sorry."

"I can tell. Anyway, even if it was weird, I still give you credit for coming over to talk to me. Everyone else seems to be afraid my disdain for status might be contagious." She shook my hand. "Tara Elspeth."

"Gordon Paget-Mann," I said, finally remembering my fake name. "So, are you in school for art?" I asked. "Or did you already finish? How did you get this gig?"

"It was sort of by accident. I had a Twitter account where I made fun of museums and galleries, and *The Hypochondriac* liked it and offered me a job writing freelance reviews. I was finishing grad school and needed the money, and *voilà*: here I am."

The security guard came back.

"You can put your bicycle in the Lessaker's personal garage," he said, as if he had just swallowed a thumb tack and was in pain.

"Great," Tara said. "Gordon, can you give me a hand?"

It took me a second to remember that I was Gordon today.

She handed me her oversized climbing backpack, and I followed her as she wheeled her bike up the driveway towards the brick house. When we got close to the three bays of the garage, the security guard muttered "We're here" into his radio and the far right door began opening. Inside were a large Chevy Suburban, a grey Tesla, and a green Jaguar.

"Ooh, look. Malcolm's work car, his wife's respectable car, and the fun car," Tara said.

"You can put your bicycle here, if that's acceptable," the security guard said, pointing to the wall next to the BMW. The garage was so clean, I wondered if rich people had maids to clean their garages as well as their houses.

Tara placed her bike against the wall and pointedly locked the wheel to the frame as if the millionaires might steal her scuffed-up old ten-speed.

"Hand me the bag," she said, and I did. She ran the strap through the lock as well, creating a big clump of bike, chain, and nylon. She took a small notebook and pen out of one of the bag's pockets.

"Now let's go see some art," she said.

SIXTEEN

We walked back towards the fountain, and the garage door closed behind us. I had clocked some motion-sensing flood lights in and outside the garage, but there were no cameras that I could discern. I filed that information away in case it came in handy later.

An uptight man had gathered the others at the fountain and smiled awkwardly at us as we arrived—clearly nobody had updated him on the bicycle situation, and he could not be sure if we were being escorted back by security because we were trouble-makers or if we were personal guests of the Lessakers coming from an insiders' tour.

"She had to put her bike in the garage," the security guard said. I caught his tone of annoyance, but the tour guide obviously didn't know what to make of this information which didn't answer his unspoken question about whether we were high- or low-status guests. He settled for a vague, friendly "Welcome!" tossed in our direction before turning his head back to the main group of museum visitors.

"As I was saying," he picked up, "you are incredibly lucky today to get to view the collection of the Lessaker Foundation."

Tara jotted down a few notes in her book.

"This collection of contemporary art is unparalleled and, I should add, admired by many of the major museums of the world. In addition to the treasures of art, you get to savor the experience, which has been planned to the smallest detail, from the landscaping and entrance, to the delicate and graceful lines of the museum building itself."

Tara rolled her eyes at me as she made notes in her book.

"If everyone is ready to begin, let us proceed to the embarkation point."

"The what?" I asked. I swear it just popped out. Tara laughed.

"The embarkation point," he repeated. "It's just this way." Since he didn't actually answer my question, I started to doubt whether he knew what it meant either. Anyway, we walked from the driveway across a bit of lawn to a concrete platform with an uncomfortable-looking bench. No one sat down. A gravel path led off over a small hill towards the museum.

Here the tour guide launched into a shorter and cleaned-up version of the biography of Malcolm Lessaker I presented earlier. He left out the misdeeds and made the man sound like Albert Schweitzer and Jonas Salk rolled up into one.

As he was talking, I peered out into the lawn, trying to see if I could spot motion-detecting lights, infrared cameras, or possibly, claymore mines.

I did not see anything like that, but did notice a deer near the boundary of the property, which led me to believe there were no such alarms in the lawn, or if there were, they had been deactivated or turned to impossibly high settings, so as to not activate for every squirrel, deer, and fox prancing across the grounds.

As the uptight man got to the end of his glorification of the Lessakers, a fleet of golf carts appeared over the hill, humming their way towards us. I heard one lady say "Ooooh." I don't know if she had never seen a golf cart before, but that seemed unlikely, so I guessed she was just delighted not to have to walk 50 feet to get to the art. Or perhaps she was impressed by the timing of the vehicles' arrival, which I will admit was rather neat. Perhaps the uptight man had some sort of signal device, or the security guard did? Then again it might have been pure luck.

"And now," he said, "if you will all board the transportation, we can make our way to the museum grounds." I noted that he constructed the sentence in a way that avoided the phrase "golf carts," which would not have conveyed the sophistication he desired.

Most of the visitors were already paired off with spouses, so Tara and I ended up sitting next to each other in the back of the last vehicle. With a slight humming sound, we started moving up the slight grade that provided a buffer between the mansion and museum.

The tour guide's voice surprised me when it came through the cart's speakers.

"As we approach, notice the landscaped hills, inspired by the hunt clubs further outside the city and terraced to provide suitable grounds for fox hunting should the neighbors ever allow it."

Tara rolled her eyes at this, and I even saw some of the presumably wealthy guests do a double-take as if they weren't sure they had heard him correctly.

"As we roll gently down into the Museum's grounds, notice the first installation, Yjork Baldog's *The Green Knight*, which provides a transition from the pastoral fields to the more constructed environs of the Lessaker."

The sculpture was a giant horse head, in the shape of a chess piece, covered in grass and flowers. You could easily envision it on a roadside mini golf course near a dying beach town, but here it was *art*, or so the guide told us.

"It captures the chivalrous splendor of the tale of Sir Gaiwin, while also posing a question about man's role in the shifting fortunes of the game of life. For if this is a knight, are we all just pawns?"

He let this question hang in the air and Tara groaned.

"You know, they're cutting corners already," she said to me. "The flowers haven't been replanted recently enough."

"Huh?"

"*The Green Knight* is supposed to be garlanded with fresh flowers once a week, according to the artist, but it looks like they only do it every two or three at most."

"Once a month," said our golf cart driver, turning his head back to us.

"They only plant flowers once a month? Geez," Tara said.

"Yes, but between you and me, they keep it spruced up with some fake flowers for color." He turned back to face the asphalt road ahead.

"Yikes," Tara said.

I noticed we were finally entering into a perimeter of electronic sensors in the lawn, although *The Green Knight* was outside it. I pointed that out to Tara.

"Well, there's no point, it's not like anyone is going to steal *The Green Knight*."

"Yeah, it's too big to put in a truck," I said.

"Also, it's too ugly to bother."

We rounded a bend and passed some small white cubes on the way to a golf cart parking lot near the museum's entrance.

"And now we have arrived. Please be aware of your surroundings. There are over 300 distinct types of flora and fauna on the Lessaker grounds, all working together in a symphonic ecosystem."

If this was how the guy talked about a suburban field, I was not sure I would survive him describing art for a couple of hours.

"Feel free to leave your bags and cellular phones in the vehicles. They will be safe, and more importantly, the entire experience has been designed to fill up 100 percent of your senses, and any electronic distractions may detract from the experience."

"Fascists," Tara said. "I'm keeping my phone."

I shrugged at her, and tossed my phone into a basket in the front seat, but got out my secret camera that was shaped like a pen.

We fell into the pack of visitors and walked towards the thick glass doors at the front of the museum. I noted the positions of the locks with minimal interest—breaking in through a glass door is for amateurs.

"Of course," the guide said, "you all probably recognized the famous piece we just passed." I certainly did not. I think he was talking about the cubes, which looked like something you could buy at The Container Store. He then mentioned the artist who made them, and I could have sworn it was one of the cast members of *Three's Company*. I was going to ask Tara about that, but I was too embarrassed.

The doors swung open for us automatically, incredibly slowly, and we entered the front lobby.

SEVENTEEN

ONCE THE DOORS CLOSED BEHIND US, IT FELT LIKE WE WERE IN a large jewelry store in the center of a newly built, high-end mall. It wasn't a comforting feeling. There was an air of expectation, as if it would reflect poorly on us if we did not appreciate the things that had been gathered here for us.

The tour guide inhaled deeply and I thought for a moment he was about to lead us in a spontaneous yoga routine. When he exhaled, he smiled with the contentment of somebody who had truly found peace and harmony in the universe, or who had just farted.

"I am proud to present to you, the Lessaker collection." He spread his hands out in a gesture towards the art, but due to the shape of the lobby, we could not see any at the time, so it seemed like he was presenting invisible art on the walls.

"If anyone needs to use the facilities, this is an excellent time to do so. Afterwards, I'll guide us on a short 30-minute tour of the highlights, and you'll have half an hour after that to revisit any part of the collection you wish."

A couple other visitors hustled towards the bathroom, while others looked around and, presumably, admired the sheetrock

walls and brass signage that said "Men's Lounge" and
"Women's Lounge."

"The thing is, the Lessakers would probably scoff at
someone who said they only spent an hour at The Met or The
Whitney," Tara said to me quietly. "Like they were tourists with
no appreciation of art. But the museum only gives us an hour
here. Which either means their collection is skimpy—and I
know it's not—or they don't really care if people have a chance
to actually engage with the art."

I was not quite sure why she had selected me as her confi-
dant, but I was happy to take the role. In turning away from
the other guests, she had also turned us so that our backs were
to the one camera in the lobby, which worked out well for me,
and I tried to keep the private conversation going.

"I once spent four full hours at the National Gallery of
Art," I told her. "Because it was raining out, and I didn't have
an umbrella. I engaged with a lot of art that day."

"I saw in an interview where the Lessakers said they didn't
put any artwork in the lobby of the museum because they did
not consider anything in their collection to be *lobby art*," she
said. "But that just means the lobby ends up being boring."

Eventually everyone finished up in the bathroom, and we
started our tour. I don't remember everything the guide said. I
made a recording of it with my spy pen, but I have never
listened to it, because I didn't need to be that bored again for
the rest of my life.

It was not that the art was bad. It just seemed like the tour
guide had found the least interesting piece of information
about every work and shared it with us.

There were no labels on the walls near the pieces like at
most museums. When someone asked about that, the guide
said the Lessakers did not want guests distracted by the text,
and since nobody was visiting the museum without getting the
tour, the wall text was unnecessary. Tara asked if there was an

exhibition catalogue available, and found out there was not. She rolled her eyes again. She had done it so much that I wondered if she was having a series of mini seizures, but when I asked, she told me that she was in perfect health.

Throughout, I noticed that there were no taped lines on the floor noting how far back one should stand, and that the guide got right next to the sculptures and paintings without setting off any sort of alarm. In one case, I'm pretty sure he accidentally touched a canvas while pointing out a detail on a portrait of a Nigerian aristocrat. He pursed his lips suddenly and pulled his finger back as he kept talking, but he didn't point directly at anything else for the rest of the tour.

There were some fountains in the middle of the museum, built in the minimalist style that looked like a leak had sprung —two marble slabs with water gargling out from the crack between them. It barely made a sound, and then the water ran down to the floor and into a gently sloped concrete trough that directed the water into a drain. Call me old fashioned, but I think a fountain should have a lady with wings, or a little chubby baby spitting, or animals or something. There shouldn't be a danger that you might accidentally sit on the fountain because you thought it was just a bench. Between the one in the driveway of his mansion and the ones in the interior of his museum, Lessaker had a horrible eye for fountains.

Just as I thought we were about to enter the last part of the museum, the tour guide mercifully announced that we had already concluded. I was glad to be done listening to him drone on about art, but I did feel a bit cheated. I pointed to the section of the building we hadn't seen yet.

"What's in there?"

"Oh, those are the administration and collections management offices. Not part of the tour, sadly."

Normally I would not want a tour of boring offices, but in this case I had hoped to sneak a peek. Perhaps, I thought, I could pretend to get lost later and open the wrong door and barge in. But then Tara chimed in.

"I'm supposed to speak with the assistant curatorial manager," she said. "She was going to show me the advanced scanning and documenting equipment they have."

"Ah, yes," said the guide. "I'll call her and see if she can meet with you."

"Actually," Tara said, "I know they're very proud of the system and would love to show it to the whole group if they're interested."

Now the tables had turned and the guide was the one rolling his eyes. "I imagine everyone would prefer to use the time to enjoy the art and grounds… "

Most of the people nodded and turned away from the office doors. But then one guy pulled back from his wife and quietly said, "That sounds kind of interesting, honey, maybe I'll do that while you look at the art." I was pretty sure I saw her throw him a dirty look that he missed as he innocently ambled over towards Tara and the guide. "I'm Colin Gorman-Grey," he said, sticking out his hand, which the guide was obliged to shake. "To be honest," he said, "I find computers more interesting than art, but don't tell Maggie that." Maggie was, presumably, his wife.

I shrugged my shoulders. "I wouldn't mind seeing the scanning and documenting equipment either," I said with all the nonchalance I could muster.

"Wouldn't you like to spend more time at the Mayslie Retepps exhibit?" The guide was starting to look suspicious. "We kind of sped past it, because some of our guests find it dated, but I was told you were writing a thesis on her work."

"I am," I lied. "But to be honest, the professor I'm having the hardest time with focuses on curatorial services, and I think I'd score more points with him if I can talk to him about the Lessakers' system."

He warily eyed the three of us, sighed, then stepped back and whispered into his radio.

"You're into computers?" I asked Colin.

"Yes," he said, then looked at the floor and put his hands in his pockets.

"I'm Tara, and I've already forgotten this guy's name. Sorry."

"I'm ... uh ... Gordon." Why could I never remember my fake name? We all shook hands and waited for the guide to return. I was sure we would be busted, or at least, I would, since I was the only one using a fake identity. I had just started to sweat when he came back.

"Miss Simms will see you now."

"Ooh, I can't wait to meet *Miss* Simms," Tara said to Colin. "I wonder if *Miss* Spinster *and Miss* Presuffragette will be there too?"

"Do they work at the museum?" he asked.

Tara laughed, and he smiled uncomfortably as if he had indeed meant to make a joke, which I think he had not.

The heavy door slowly opened via hydraulics, and a woman in a sweater and jeans walked towards us, taking off white cotton gloves and removing her goggles.

"Lauren Simms, assistant curatorial manager," she said. After stuffing the thin gloves into her pocket she shook our hands. "I was only expecting one, but I'm happy to give you all a look."

"Just give me a call when you're done, and I can pick them up," the tour guide said.

"No problem, Wayne," Lauren said.

He walked back towards the museum.

"Goodbye, Wayne," Tara said. Somehow she made his name sound like an insult. He didn't turn around, though, as the door closed with a quiet hissing sound.

EIGHTEEN

"WELCOME TO THE BRAINS OF THE OPERATION," LAUREN SAID. "The Lessakers have an extensive collection of art and also display works on loan from other institutions, and we're responsible for cataloguing and tracking all of it."

She picked up a small white scanner that looked like a prop from one of the new *Star Trek* movies.

"Obviously, inventory and management is a big part of the pharmaceutical industry, and the Lessaker Museum has leveraged the family's connections to build a completely new, proprietary database system more advanced than any other in the art world."

Lauren walked along and expected us to follow, but Tara did not move and instead asked a question.

"Is the system as vulnerable to exploitation as the opioid painkiller market?"

This stopped Lauren.

"I thought you were writing about art and the museum."

"I'm writing about the whole enterprise," Tara said.

Lauren's smile melted away.

"I can direct you to the PR department if you'd like to talk about that sort of thing further."

"That'd be great," Tara said.

"I'd still like to hear about the computers," Colin mumbled. "If that's okay."

"Well, let's finish the tour then," Lauren said. "No more opioid talk, though."

"Mum's the word," Tara said.

Lauren resumed walking, and led us towards a metal sculpture of a chunky metal face with a big forehead. She turned to face us like an angry school teacher.

"Can anyone tell me what this sculpture is?"

"Looks like a lesser Brancusi," Tara said.

Lauren pulled a white glove out of her pocket, put it on her left hand, and tilted the sculpture up from the base, then scanned the bottom of it with the device until there was a beeping sound from the scanner and her pocket. Then she lowered the sculpture and removed a phone from her pocket.

"I've not only brought up all the relevant information on this piece, but the scan itself was recorded, so we keep a meticulous history of where the art is at all times and a chain of custody as well."

"Um, why do you need the scanner if your phone has a QR code reader?" Colin asked.

"Excellent question," Lauren said, smiling again. "We would not entrust our collection to the operating system of a smartphone, which is vulnerable to outside attacks. The scanner is linked into a proprietary communications network that transmits on a secure link to our database, then patches the information to my phone."

"Is the database housed here?"

"Unfortunately, I am not at liberty to discuss that."

"Can I scan something?" Colin asked, sounding as giddy as a child about to blow out the candles on his birthday cake.

"I think we can arrange that."

It seemed like Colin was having the time of his life as he took the scanner. Lauren led us a bit further back towards some big wooden crates. First she had him scan a piece of paper on a desk, which she said logged in their location, then let him scan the QR codes on the sides of some of the crates. He squealed with glee each time, and as we bounced around the facility following him scanning, I tried to roll my eyes to Tara but she seemed to have slipped away momentarily. Eventually we got to another set of crates which were roped off with that flimsy pink tape they use to mark construction sites sometimes.

"I think we'll stop here," Lauren said.

"That's fine. These crates don't have anything to scan," Colin said. "Well, this was really fun, thank you." Then he gritted his teeth and said, "You've really made my day." I think he was trying to do a Clint Eastwood impression, but it was not very good. He blew into the end of the scanner like it was a revolver he had just fired, then tried to swivel the scanner around in his hand like a cowboy would twirl a pistol, but he didn't have the dexterity to do it, and besides, the scanner lacked a trigger guard to catch on his index finger, so it went flying into the air.

Lauren's eyes bugged out and she might have even shrieked as it flew through the air and clattered into an employee's desk.

"I'm sorry!" Colin yelled and ran towards it.

"That's OK, just leave it," Lauren said sharply. She walked over to the desk and picked up the scanner, examining it like she was appraising an antique teapot. "I don't think it's damaged," she said at last.

"Those things are pretty sturdy," Tara said, walking towards us from the unmarked crates.

"Well, they're built to withstand the wear and tear of a CVS pharmacist who doesn't know what they're doing."

"I'm sorry, again," Colin said. His smile had disappeared and he once again wore the beaten down expression he'd had when standing next to his wife.

"Why don't we just head back to the museum for now," Lauren said, herding us back towards the door where we had first entered.

Re-entering the museum space, Lauren told us we had about 15 minutes left of our experience, then closed the door behind us and went back to her job.

"That's not very much time for a museum, is it?" I asked.

"Not for a real museum, anyway," Tara said.

"Well, I should find my wife. I would, um, appreciate it if we didn't … I mean … she doesn't need to know about how I dropped the scanner in there. Good to meet you both."

With that, he shuffled off towards the rear of the gallery and the doors to the outdoor space.

"Do you mind if I mention you in my review? I want to make it clear it wasn't just me who had a bone to pick with this place, but that another visitor felt the same way."

"Sure, please don't describe me as the guy going through a midlife crisis, though."

"I wouldn't think of it. And I'll be sure to give you a fake name, *Gordon Paget-Mann*." She said it as if she knew that one was already made up. Well, as long as she didn't use my real name, I would be fine.

"Have a good rest of your trip. Be safe on that bicycle."

I walked in the same direction Colin had gone, wanting to check out the back lawn of the museum and find out if there were any additional security measures in place there.

———

I WILL ADMIT THERE WAS A PLEASANT SET OF WELL-SCULPTED green hills, and I felt my heart rate settle back down after the excitement of the insider's tour.

I walked around and enjoyed the art as much as I could. At one point, I thought I saw a security camera in the grass, but it turned out to be a small sculpture of a security camera that was, I guess, making a commentary on the surveillance state, or something.

My favorite part of the museum was a wall full of small paintings by Lottye Kugeios. Each was of a window and the view of the countryside through the window. The land in the distance was always a bit disturbing. Perhaps as a thief, I was drawn to the representation of windows, which I often used to enter buildings. I don't know enough about art to explain why, but I really loved these small paintings. The one I liked the most seemed to be a window in a castle with thick stone walls, and in the distance was a mountaintop, shining in the moonlight, almost as if it was made of gold. I couldn't tell what it was called because there were no labels on the wall. I would have to look it up online later.

If this place was *truly* open to the public, it would be a nice sort of museum, smaller and more intimate than the big names, but more personal. It wasn't though. Open to the public, I mean. After just a few minutes of my reverie, we were all called back to the museum by Wayne the tour guide.

"I hope you enjoyed your visit to the Lessaker Museum," he said. Then he began handing out leaflets. "The Lessaker Foundation is a non-profit dedicated to preserving and enhancing great works of contemporary art for the ages. If you would like to make a contribution, the attached form has all the relevant information. Your gifts help make our continued existence possible. Thank you, and I hope you have a wonderful rest of your day."

I looked at my watch. We hadn't even gotten a full hour.

The security guard was locking the glass doors of the entrance as we got back into the golf carts. We were the first tour of the day, and also the last. On top of that, this billionaire had the audacity to ask me for donations to help fund his private backyard art gallery.

Although Tara and I had said goodbye earlier, we hopped into the same golf cart again.

Halfway back to the house, the whole caravan pulled off the drive, creating small tire tracks on the previously well-manicured lawn.

"Just one moment," came Wayne's voice through the speakers. "There's a bit of a traffic jam."

Then another cart came towards us from the house. Malcolm Lessaker himself was driving, with a large man I didn't recognize in the passenger seat. In the back, two women were chatting amiably. As they passed, they completely ignored all of us, continuing at a slow speed, taking their sweet time.

It was as close as I ever came to the man.

After they had passed, our large collection of vehicles was allowed back on the roadway and we resumed our trip to the mansion. Tara and I both looked back to see that Malcolm had parked his golf cart crookedly right in front of the glass doors, which he was opening with his own set of keys, then the road curved away and we could no longer see him.

"Do you know who those people with the Lessakers were?" I asked Tara.

"No idea. To be honest, I didn't even recognize the Lessakers. I don't read *Vanity Fair* or whatever."

"The other couple is from Georgia," said our driver. "But not the state in America, they're from the country in Russia. They've been here a few times already this month. I guess they don't have art where they live. It's kind of annoying because there's a whole bunch of extra security they bring with them when they show up."

After a bit of silence, we arrived at the concrete platform with the uncomfortable looking bench.

"Ah, yes, good to be back at the embarkation point," I said.

Tara laughed. "It's actually the debarkation point now."

"That's weird," I said, "it looks exactly like the embarkation point."

We both thanked the driver and headed towards the garage to get her bike. We did not get very far before two men built and dressed like bodyguards stepped out to block our way.

"I left my bike in the garage," she told them.

One of the men whispered into a comms device on his wrist in another language. Wayne and the security guard ran over to us.

"Sorry for the confusion," Wayne said. "We just need to get her bicycle out of the garage."

"We're not supposed to let anyone in the house," said the bodyguard on the left.

"Yeah," added the bodyguard on the right.

"We're not going into the house, just the garage," Tara said.

"I'll handle this," the security guard said to Tara. Then he turned to the bodyguards and said, "We're not going into the house, just the garage."

"Pardon. Do you require some assistance?" said a new voice with a bad French accent.

We all turned around and saw my driver, the improv comedian, who winked at me. "Bon jour! Je m'appelle Chad!"

Everyone ignored him.

Tara just started walking towards the garage. The bodyguards looked to the security guard, who shrugged and said, "Don't cause a scene." Then he spoke into his radio and the garage door started opening. I hurried over to help her with her bag. My driver followed along, muttering "mais oui" and "comme ci, comme ca."

By the time I got to the garage, though, Tara had already slung the bag onto her back and gotten on the bike.

"Gentlemen, it's been a pleasure," she said to the guards. Then she nodded at me. "See you around, Gordon."

With that, she pedaled off into the night.

"Au revoir!" yelled my driver after her, as I tugged his arm towards our car, and the security guard had the garage door closed behind us.

Once in the car, I had to listen to his improv all the way back to the city, as well as his off-key renditions of some songs that I assume were from *Les Miz*, and I began to regret most of the choices I had made in life.

NINETEEN

Now it was time to get to work.

A prosecutor might suggest that this is when the conspirators gathered to put their nefarious plans into action. I would prefer to say that this is when the group of friends with mutual interests began hanging out more frequently.

The place where Fiona was staying was not an ideal headquarters, since we would technically be storing evidence of future crimes, and the owners could change their plans and suddenly return home at any time. So I got us an office at a coworking space in Washington, D.C.

This made sense for a few reasons. There is a lot of turnover at those places, and as soon as we were done, they would give the room a thorough cleaning for the next client, getting rid of our fingerprints and DNA for us. Also, they would probably not want the bad PR of their business being used as a home base for a felony, and would therefore do their best to cover up our tracks if the police came calling. Last but not least, there was a fully stocked kitchen and free beer. The only drawback was that everyone else who worked there was insufferable.

Keisha created a fake website for our company, and even came up with a supposed app we were building, ArtLocatr, which I did not fully understand. I think it crowdsourced works of art by GPS so you could easily find all the paintings by a specific person in a five mile radius. Anyway, it made a good cover story for all the art resources in our office space.

The guy who had been cheating on his wife on the train to New Hampshire unknowingly opened up a new credit card account through the folks at Wells Fargo, who did not do a thorough background check, and that card paid for our expenses at the co-working space.

In heist movies, this portion of the planning is usually covered in a montage, which makes sense because it's a lot of details and paperwork, which isn't the most thrilling thing to watch on the big screen.

The basic gist of the plan was pretty simple: we were going to rob the place twice.

First, we would disguise ourselves as an art handling company, and, taking advantage of the lax security measures, steal the works we wanted and replace them with forgeries created by one of my associates (specifically, the one I used to date, named Josie). Here, the fact that the museum was rarely open to guests worked in our favor. In an actual museum, a guest was likely to spot the reproduction at some point. In this case, very few legitimate art enthusiasts would see our fakes.

Then, several months later, we would rob the place again, only this job would get intentionally botched, leaving most of the replica paintings on the walls, and some of them damaged. At this point, when the Lessakers activated their insurance, the world would discover that most of his collection was actually fakes. By targeting works he had collected over a long period of time from different sellers and auctions, we could create the implication that the forgeries had been created in his museum over the years, as opposed to him having accidentally bought a few fakes. That would create a bigger market for paintings that had once been in his collection, since the provenance was now in doubt and everyone knew the originals were out in the world somewhere.

There were still a few details to work out, but that was the general gist. The biggest issue was that it changed the timeline. New Year's still seemed like the best time for a flashy job, so that meant we had to do the quiet switch before then. The other reason for that was that it would be difficult to fake a big delivery during a holiday, so it had to happen sooner. The few days before Thanksgiving seemed like a good option, since it was technically a work week but people let their guard down, staffs were light due to travel, and then everyone ate themselves into lethargic food comas afterward.

That gave us the schedule.

The other thing we had to figure out was: who were those two guests with the bodyguards at the mansion? It was easy enough to figure out the general calendar of the museum and plan around it, but if Lessaker was doing side deals, we might get caught off-guard by him and his buyers showing up during the job. On top of that, if he was dealing with gangsters, things could turn violent. Mob men, whether they're American or Russian, tend not to forgive the people who steal from them, no matter how charming, handsome, or well-intentioned they may be.

While Fiona tried to get more information about Lessaker's guests that day, Keisha continued working on the security system. The first job, replacing the real paintings with fakes, represented more of a challenge for her, since we needed to cover our tracks and make it look like nothing had happened. For the second robbery, we wanted to make a splash, so as long as our identities were protected, we did not care if the act was recorded on their cameras and sensors, what little of them the museum had.

IT'S THE LITTLE THINGS THAT GET YOU THROUGH IN A LOT OF situations.

If a guy shows up in an electric company van with an electric company uniform and he knows your name, you're likely to let him in to look at your meter. But if he shows up in an old Ford Taurus, wearing a t-shirt, and asks your name, you are right to be suspicious.

In reality, these days, a lot of full-time employees with uniforms and company vehicles have been replaced by temporary workers and freelancers. Packages are delivered by random people unaffiliated with any official service. The person who shows up to install your cable is some weirdo they found on the internet. Companies don't want to hire full-time employees and give them benefits because that comes out of the executives' pay and bonuses. Nevertheless, our brains haven't caught up with the new economy, and we still give a free pass to a well-uniformed employee, even if that's actually a less likely sight in the present day.

Which meant we needed to get a realistic art handling company truck. It had to be in good shape, too. We couldn't just slap a decal onto some old rundown van or dying delivery vehicle. At the same time, stealing a truck from Crozier's, or one of their competitors, could set off too many alarms in the art community and put people on their toes.

Fiona came up with the idea of using Lessaker's own trucks against him. His pharmaceutical companies made deliveries all over the country, which meant we did not need to take one from near our target. And if one of his trucks was stolen, the authorities would probably assume it was some addict or dealer trying to get their hands on some opioids.

The current overdose capitals in America are New Hampshire and Kentucky, so we decided to get a truck from New

Hampshire. Josie lived nearby in Vermont, which would be helpful, and on top of that, I did not want to ever go to Kentucky.

TWENTY

A LOT OF NEW HAMPSHIRE WAS RUST AND SALVAGE COUNTRY. Junkyards full of overgrown tractors wedged between maple syrup farms and sugar shacks, cars stacked on top of cars, old buses on their sides with grass growing through the broken windows. This was where we went.

The college near Josie had been decorated with neatly manicured ivy. But in other parts of the state, buildings are losing the war to weeds. I took a bus to Manchester and rented a junker of a car from a guy named Don that I found on Craigslist. It wasn't too long of a walk from the bus station.

He lived in a small brown house a few blocks back from Canal Street. I knocked, then heard him yelling from inside.

"I'll be there, hold on."

I had tried to make an appointment, but he said he was home all day, I should just stop by. His voice sounded grizzled and worn, one of those dying breeds of life-long smokers. The next generation will have life-long vapers. I heard him bump his way to the door, and it finally opened.

His face was just what I expected, sturdy and leathery, but his hair surprised me, it was dyed pink, which was unusual given that he was in his late 60s and lived in New Hampshire. I had washed all the pink dye out of my own hair by this point.

"Hey, you must be the guy about the car," he said to me. "Come on in."

I followed him back through deep stacks of old newspapers piled in the mudroom into his living room, where he threw himself into a worn fabric couch. He picked up a pack of cigarettes from the beat-up wooden coffee table and lit one. After he had been smoking it in silence for about a minute, he said, "Do you mind if I smoke?"

"Go ahead," I told him.

He propped his feet up on the table, and I saw an ankle monitor on the bottom of his right leg.

"Yeah, so I drove into a house, which is why I can't use the car for a while. Don't worry, nobody was killed. But they said I was drunk, so no more driving for Don."

He hopped up from the couch, spry for his age. Maybe the cigarette had renewed his energy. He disappeared down a hallway and came back with a stack of newspapers.

"Here it is!"

He threw the stack on the floor at my feet, and I saw a headline, *Driver Plows Into Mobile Home*. There was half a picture of a truck in the broken living room of a house before it disappeared under the fold of the paper.

"You would have thought they could bury it inside, out of loyalty. But I guess the photo was too good."

He gestured to a chair near the coffee table.

"Have a seat. I'd like to get to know you a little before I give you my car."

I gave him a mostly true description of my life. I told him I had recently been laid off from my job managing an AC repair school and decided that rather than sit around at home feeling sorry for myself, I'd come check out the foliage of New England, which I'd always meant to do but never found the time. Because I was without a job, though, I was on a budget, and renting a car from him was cheaper than using an actual car rental service.

"I guess that makes sense," he said. "But I'll tell you right now, if you get up to no good with my car, I'll report it stolen and claim I don't know you. I'll say I didn't know it was stolen at first because I'm under house arrest." He tapped his ankle bracelet, then tapped his head to show he had thought it through already.

"Rest easy, Don. I'm not going to rob a bank in your car." And I meant it, I wasn't going to rob a bank. I was merely going to steal a truck. "If you don't mind me asking, how did you get an ankle bracelet just for drunk driving? Don't they usually just put a breathalyzer on your car?"

"Yeah, well, I left the scene of the crime, for one. And it was the D.A.'s house, so I think they had it in for me."

"The district attorney lives in a trailer?"

"Welcome to New Hampshire. Anyway, I left my truck in his living room and walked away, so they think I'm a flight risk."

He coughed a bit and then offered me a drink, which I declined.

"Oh, I forgot to tell you. I should have said when you showed up. I used to work for the newspaper. I managed the printing press at night and drove bundles of paper to a few pick-ups out of town. After work, I'd be so tired that I brought leftover stacks back here instead of going by the dump. That's what all this mess is." He gestured at all the stacks of newspapers. "Just so you don't think I'm a hoarder."

"I had been wondering about that," I said.

He walked over toward the kitchen and came back with a keychain.

"Here you go." He held it out to me. "She ain't the best car in the world, but she gets the job done."

I pulled an envelope full of cash out of my pocket and handed it to him in exchange for the key.

"It's parked about three blocks down that way," he said, pointing off away from town. "It's the one with the bundles of newspapers in the back seat, and the front is scratched up from when I drove into the district attorney's trailer."

"I may need to unload the papers if I want to use the back seat," I said.

"You can just throw them away. Or recycle them if you're one of those hippies. I don't need them back."

"Thanks, Don," I said.

"My pleasure."

"One more thing," I said, lingering in his hallway.

"My pink hair?"

"Yes."

"My son bet me $50 I wouldn't do it. I never turned down a dare in my life. Plus I needed the money. It don't look too bad, huh?"

He laughed, and I left him there chuckling to himself.

TWENTY-ONE

THERE'S A COUPLE OF WAYS TO STEAL A TRUCK.

You can use brute force, hijacking it. You can wait until it's unattended and make off with it (a variation of that is to replace the stolen truck with a similar truck so the owner doesn't notice immediately). You could possibly tow it away if you have a big enough tow truck.

In this case, the problem was that the truck would be guarded the whole time, almost like an armored car making cash pickups and deliveries. In a way, a truck full of drugs is more valuable than a truck full of cash. But it's better to steal money, because you can turn around and spend it. Stealing drugs requires a lot of effort down the road, because you have to sell the drugs to make a profit, so common criminals are more apt to rob a bank truck.

I was not a common criminal.

Keisha was able to find a backdoor into a New Hampshire health insurance company computer system that gave her a delivery schedule for certain TravMG/Lessaker pharmaceuticals. I followed some trucks around for a couple days to verify the info, and soon we had a good sense of when the trucks went where. And on top of that, I knew when they had their defenses up and down.

The crew of an armored bank car is most alert and watchful when making a delivery, because the door to the truck is open at the same time as the door to the vault. A well-timed hit then could clear out the truck and the bank.

In the case of drug deliveries, a similar logic was at work. When they were making pick-ups and deliveries, they were most vulnerable since they had to open the back of the truck, which was a complicated process. And on top of that, the storage facilities of the hospital, or pharmacy supply chain, would also be open.

Conversely, the drivers and guards were most at ease immediately after a successful delivery—once the moment of danger passed, their adrenaline levels plummeted and they crashed. It's like the disappearance of a sugar rush—suddenly they are not only at ease, but well below it, making their reflexes slow, their suspicions too slight.

There were a few different truck sizes, and I wanted one big enough to fill with art, but not so big that it would raise eyebrows driving through the ritzy North Potomac suburbs. It needed to be small enough that no one would remember it later.

Of the trucks on the route, one fit that description. It ran deliveries along Route 93, running diagonally northwest and southeast out of Manchester. Its two-man crew stopped at a diner just off the highway at the start of their service every morning, right after they left the overnight lot, and grabbed some donuts and to-go coffees, before driving half a mile to stock up at the TravMG supply warehouse. After that, they got on the highway and pulled off at every major exit to make drops, mostly at pain clinics and big chain pharmacies.

In theory, I could hit the empty truck in the morning, but that might be too strange. While police would accept that some junkie or dealer with initiative accidentally hit an empty truck, they would expect to find that truck abandoned nearby as soon as the thieves realized they'd screwed up. With a truck *full* of opioids, the authorities would not be surprised to see it vanish into thin air. In reality, if I was stealing the truck to get at the drugs, I would ditch the truck as soon as possible and move the cargo into storage or another vehicle. But people stealing pain medication aren't always thinking straight, and the police could reasonably expect them to keep driving the truck until they got as far away from the scene of the crime as possible.

————

THE NIGHT BEFORE THE JOB, I BROKE INTO THE BLUE DOT Diner and replaced their main supply of coffee with decaf. (My apologies to any of the diner's regulars who felt drowsy that day as a result.)

I also found the Blue Dot's donut supplier and dosed that day's order with melatonin. To prevent accidents and a widespread epidemic of drowsiness in town, I stopped by the diner at the same time as the drug truck and bought up all the donuts remaining after the TravMG employee bought his, pretending to be a flustered businessman who overslept and forgot to get donuts for a morning meeting at a hotel. I had considered that a flustered parent trying to bring donuts to a student event would be more sympathetic, but worried that the diner employees would know every school and parent in town and notice that I was out of place. It was a shame because they were delicious donuts—I had tried an un-dosed one during my surveillance a few days earlier.

My flustered business man act also served as a diversion to distract the man from the TravMG truck while he was loading cream and sugar into his coffee and the coffee for his driver. I slipped a dose of the Rohypnol I had stolen from the fraternity on my previous trip to New Hampshire into both of his cups and then watched him stir the drug in with a wooden stick before walking back to his truck.

———

THERE WAS AN ACCESS ROAD LEADING OUT OF THE INDUSTRIAL park where their supply warehouse was located. A long time ago, someone had installed a gate that could be lowered to close the parking lot. Perhaps they were having problems with teens doing drugs (or doing each other) in parked cars there after hours. In any case, it was supposed to be open every morning when the factory opened. I guessed there were times the trucks got there before the gate was open and it wouldn't make them too suspicious to see it closed.

The day I took the truck, the gate was open when they arrived, but closed when they tried to leave. The drivers were almost asleep by the time they finished their pick-up, having filled the back of their truck with drugs. I saw one rubbing his eyes repeatedly through my binoculars. The donuts were drugged. The coffee was drugged even more. There was no caffeine in their system, just melatonin and flunitrazepam.

On their way out of the warehouse parking lot, they came to the gate, which I had lowered by hand after Keisha dropped me off. The driver had to wake up the guy in the passenger seat, who got out to open it. As he was doing that, he passed out in the grass next to the road. At the same time, the driver himself nodded off. It was easy to get him out of the truck, where both their cell phones were still charging. I lowered the driver into the grass next to his buddy for a nice long nap.

I closed the gate and locked it with a heavy bike lock I'd liberated from an overpriced storefront in Brooklyn.

Then I drove away.

TWENTY-TWO

I DID NOT GO VERY FAR. A TRUCK IS LIKE A MOVING BILLBOARD, and easy for state patrolmen or the DEA to find, if it's on the road. So it was important to change the outer surface of the truck to disguise it, and at the same time remove any tracking devices that would help TravMG/Lessaker Pharmaceuticals locate their property.

Keisha met me in an unused textile mill a few miles away. She had driven there in Don's car from the drug warehouse. She was able to remove the truck's GPS and Lessaker locator. In addition, all the pills in the back were in small boxes with tracking chips.

"They're mostly used for internal tracking," she said. "They don't broadcast a signal that could be traced. But they still track back to the drugs we stole, so we should put them to sleep."

While she deactivated all the RFID chips and Josie gave the truck a makeover, I drove the men's cell phones and GPS up Route 93 to the Hooksett rest area in Don's car.

I found a pick-up truck with a confederate flag bumper sticker on its rear window underneath a gun rack. It's a weird juxtaposition to see a flag that fought for slavery on the same vehicle as a license plate that says *Live Free or Die*. I tucked the GPS tracker under an oilcloth in the truck bed and wedged the Lessaker drivers' cell phones into a crack near the back bumper.

Then I stopped inside the rest area for some ice cream, and picked up a few pies to take back to everyone at the textile mill. I sat on a bench enjoying my double scoop and watched the pick-up truck to make sure it hit the road again. Sure enough, in about 20 minutes a guy with a big beard came out, licking his fingers, and got in the truck, then drove towards the north-bound exit. When the police eventually got into the act, they would check the transponder and look north of Manchester for the stolen truck. Even if they retraced its route and found our temporary hideout, we'd be long gone, having left no finger-prints or traces.

I had to take 93 north to the small town of Bow before I could turn around and head south again, back to the textile mill.

If you have the choice between arriving somewhere with pie or without pie, always show up *with* pie. Back at the shop, Keisha and Josie had almost finished repainting the truck.

"I've got a combination of things going on, Brady," Josie explained. "First, we used a decal to replace the TravMG logo with a made-up one for a logistics company, which sounds pretty boring and should prevent anyone from taking an interest in the truck. Then we added a few bits of graffiti to make it look like a it's been on the streets for several years."

The side of the truck now said *Tech-Pro Logistics*.

"I can't see any graffiti," I said.

"We painted over it, because the fake logistics company presumably maintains their fleet of trucks pretty well."

"It may be too subtle for this lighting," Keisha said. She pointed to a spot on the side of the truck where I could now see that someone had spray-painted something, which had then been painted over with a slightly different color of white than the truck's original color.

"We should take the pie outside," Josie said. "These fumes are a bit disgusting."

In the weeds of the parking lot, there was a forgotten picnic bench where factory workers once ate lunch. We arranged the pies and sat in the late summer air, enjoying pieces of blueberry and custard pie.

The leaves had not started changing color yet, but soon they would, and the roads would get clogged with seasonal tourists, driving by for a glimpse of the fiery oranges trees, looking only upward, and ignoring the weary storefronts edging along the highway, the fading businesses and industry that were absorbing so much of the nation's supply of painkillers.

When we finished eating, we collected all our trash and put it in the trunk of Don's car, along with the stolen pills and left-over paperwork from the truck. We left nothing in the old textile mill, and just to be safe, sprinkled a fair amount of bird seed around the areas we had been in, to bury any trace evidence beneath the tracks and droppings of migratory birds.

In a small caravan of two vehicles, we drove up 93 to the White Mountains, where we found a private campsite and burned almost all the evidence in a fire using Don's stacks of newspapers from the backseat as kindling and fuel.

Josie had brought snacks and supplies to make s'mores, so we sat on stumps around the perimeter of the fire, trying to roast our marshmallows perfectly, losing bits of chocolate into the fire, burning our mouths with too-hot treats.

I've never actually enjoyed a s'more. They're too much effort. Give me a cookie any day of the week.

THEN IT WAS JUST A MATTER OF RETURNING DON'S CAR, stopping by Josie's, and driving the truck south towards Maryland. The TravMG vehicle was on the small side, like a big U-Haul you would rent to move your kid into college if you only owned an economy car. Bigger trucks required different licenses and were more likely to be pulled over. This truck was hardly noticeable. And besides, Keisha had replaced the phone number on the back that drivers were supposed to call to report unsafe conditions or behavior. If anyone tried to get the truck's driver in trouble, Keisha would dutifully take their complaint and then do absolutely nothing with it.

We stopped at a grocery store and bought a bunch of packs of bottled water, which we put in the now-empty back section of the truck. For some reason, nobody is suspicious when they find a truck driving water from one place to another. It's a horrible waste of resources, but happens so often that authorities just shrug their shoulders and move on to the next vehicle. Hopefully they would not keep searching and discover the pills now hidden in the truck's cab.

The next morning, I returned Don's car. The same parking spot I'd taken it from was empty, so I parked it there. When I told him I had gotten rid of most of the newspapers from his car, he thanked me. I walked towards a big parking lot where Josie and Keisha were going to pick me up. I grabbed a local newspaper from a drugstore and looked for an article about the prescription drug robbery.

I was a little worried it would be on the front page since it was a small town without many big news stories. But opioid thefts must have been plentiful, as it was buried in the police blotter inside the paper. *Drivers Questioned In Daylight Truck Heist.* There was no sketch of me, thankfully, just a number for the public to call if they had any information. I made note of the tip line so Keisha could bombard it with made-up tips using secure phone lines over the course of the next week, in order to distract the authorities.

I was wishing I'd brought a hat when the truck pulled up next to me at the meeting point.

"Need a lift, sir?"

"Yes, please," I said.

Josie mimed pulling on the truck's horn with her fist. "Toot toot!" Thankfully she did not actually blow the horn, which would have drawn attention.

Keisha had to get out of the passenger side to let me in.

"I already called shotgun," she said.

"And I am in charge of music," Josie added.

I was stuck in the middle, listening to Adele all the way to White River Junction.

————

"WHAT'S IT LIKE, HAVING A REAL JOB?" KEISHA ASKED JOSIE.

"It honestly has its ups and downs," Josie said. "Although I should make clear that I do not have a real job in the traditional sense. I teach a few classes a week, but I have the rest of my time off. For capers like this."

"When I was doing it," I said, "it felt like an okay tradeoff. It sucks being on the clock, but the security of a regular paycheck is great. Knowing when the money is coming and that it's going to be there."

"Until it's not there."

"Yeah, that's how they get you. I think we may have missed living in the era when a job was a permanent thing you did from high school until you stopped working, like it was for the Boomers."

"Really, truly, if I think about it," Josie said, "my career is forgery and theft. The academic work is just a … "

"Side hustle?"

"Ah yes. That's what my students call it."

"But usually," Keisha said, "a side hustle is what you're passionate about, and the other thing is your day job."

"Hmm, well. Art is my passion. Teaching it brings me as much joy as creating it. But I could never survive just as an adjunct art professor. It doesn't pay well enough."

"Forgery is your bread and butter," I said.

"I'm more sophisticated than that, Brady. Forgery is my rustic bread and olive oil."

Adele sang about heartbreak.

———

AT JOSIE'S PLACE, WE LOADED HER PAINTINGS—FORGERIES OF the dozen Lottye Kugeios paintings I had liked at the Lesser Museum—into the back of the truck, along with a few furniture pieces Josie did not need, just to make the truck look less suspicious. Anyone neighbor watching would just think someone was moving in or moving out. We were close enough to a college town that it was a common occurrence.

After my tour of the Lessaker Museum, I had looked up the paintings online to find out more about them (and discovered that the one I particularly liked was called *The Discovery of Vertigo*). Calling from a payphone in New York to a payphone in Vermont, I was able to tell Josie all about the works, and she was able to find enough information through her art world connections to create the duplicates for us.

Once the truck was loaded, we said goodbye for the time being, and Keisha and I drove south, along interstate 91, a scenic route following along the Connecticut River as it cut through the hills of Vermont.

Everything had gone according to plan so far. I had not the least inkling that I would soon have a gun pointed at me by a man who intended to use it.

TWENTY-THREE

IT WAS THE TUESDAY BEFORE THANKSGIVING. WEDNESDAY would have seemed too suspicious out in the suburbs where the Lessakers lived. In the city, there was always activity that day, people finishing up some work before the long weekend. But out where the rich leisure class lived, nobody had to work for a living, and Wednesday was dead. The holiday essentially started Tuesday afternoon.

We had replaced the Tech-Pro Logistics decal on the truck with the logo of a prominent art shipping company that often handled and inspected works for the Lessaker Museum.

Keisha added a shipping company appointment into the museum's calendar just before we arrived, in case anyone thought to check. She also hid the event from anyone not working that day—if any workaholics logged in remotely, we did not want them to see a surprise appointment they had not planned for popping up in their electronic calendar.

Smartphones have made many elements of thievery much easier. People trust everything they see on them. And Keisha says replacing the security camera feed on an image being viewed remotely is much easier than one on a closed-circuit system, which used to involve cutting a cord and replacing it with split second timing while a guard's attention was diverted.

Not to mention that everyone is permanently distracted by their phones now. People are less likely to look up and see something out of the ordinary, as long as you keep a low profile. The drawback is that everyone is carrying a camera around with them at all times, so if something goes wrong, there will be lots of video evidence for the prosecutors.

In any case, it was a skeleton crew at the museum that Tuesday afternoon. One security guard and one curatorial assistant. But Lauren Simms was on vacation already, and this security guard had not worked on the day I last visited the museum, so he wouldn't recognize me.

We called from the truck to tell them we were a few miles away and needed better directions. They told us to use the service entrance and gave us specific instructions to find it.

"It's a bit of a dirt road, but you should be fine since it hasn't rained in a while," the security guard told us. "Do you think it will take you long?"

"No, we just have to do a few re-hangings and condition checks," Keisha said. "We want to get home as badly as you do."

"I'm supposed to spend the holidays at my wife's brother's house, so I don't mind if you keep me here late. It's quieter, and I get overtime."

He laughed, and we laughed too, out of politeness.

"Don't worry, we won't tell your in-laws what time we finish," Keisha said. "See you soon."

She and I gave each other the once over. We had disguised ourselves a bit, nothing too over-the-top. I had a gross handle-bar mustache, which seemed like a cartoonish disguise, but was popular among the younger men in the art world. I had seen a few guys sporting them when I hung out with the art handlers.

Hopefully I gave off the vibe of an older worker trying to look as young as his colleagues.

Keisha had her hair in tight braids. We both wore baseball caps with the shipping company's logo on them. As long as we did not look too much like we had on our previous visits, we would be fine. We did not expect to run into anyone who had been working then, and Keisha would bypass the cameras remotely before we got out of the truck to make sure there would be no video footage of us for someone to check later.

We pulled up to an ugly industrial security gate that made the landscaped suburb look like a storage unit. I leaned out and pressed the intercom button.

"Hey, we're from the art handling company. We called a few minutes ago."

"Hello. Your other truck just pulled in. We'll re-open the gate."

Other truck?

I closed the window as we waited for the gate to open.

"They didn't have anything else on the schedule today, did they?"

"No," Keisha said. "And if they added anything last minute, I would have been notified." She was looking at a small laptop and shaking her head. "There's nothing else here."

There was no choice but to drive toward the museum and see what I had gotten us into.

"Want to jump out now?" I asked. "You can avoid any trouble."

"I'm in this, Brady. All the way in."

The gate had finally swung open and we rolled forward along the asphalt, which gave way to dirt. The service road hugged a forest on the right and a grassy field on the left.

Coming around the edge of the woods, we could see the

back of the museum, and a similar art handling truck, presumably an authentic one, parked near a service door.

"Hmm. If they challenge us, let's bluff and say we were sent over without the work order, which is going to be emailed to us later. So we don't know what job we're doing and don't have the paperwork."

"Or," Keisha said, "we could say they sent us with additional instructions beyond their work order."

"Either way, someone's going to have a lot of questions and want to call the office."

I backed the truck into a space next to the first truck.

"If they ask to see what's in the back of our truck, we may need to make a break for it. That's evidence that could get us in serious trouble."

"Understood."

"Let's make sure all the cameras are off."

"Working on it."

She frowned, looking at her laptop monitor.

"What's wrong?"

"Looks like the whole network is already down."

"Maybe they're doing some sort of repairs?"

"Possible. But unlikely."

"Can you make sure it stays down? We don't want the cameras turning back on when we're halfway through our felony."

"Give me a second."

She typed some things into her keyboard.

"Okay, that should do for now. The cameras are rerouted to send their feeds to our truck. We'll broadcast old loops to the main server in case someone turns it back on. It will work for now, but if someone sets their mind to it, they could probably figure out what I'm doing if they know where to look."

"That's as good as we're going to get." I pulled on my gloves. "Let's go have some fun!" I said. It did not feel very fun at that point. It was quite worrisome, to be honest, but I wanted to be an inspirational leader to Keisha. I had read about encouraging people in a management resource book I stole from a Border's bookstore when it still existed.

She stuffed her laptop into a shoulder bag and put on her gloves. We got out of the truck.

The service door was wedged open with a rubber door stop. I thought I should go in first, but Keisha jumped in ahead of me.

"Hello?"

"We're in here," said a voice from the administration offices I had seen during my tour.

Keisha and I shrugged at each other and walked that way. The heavy hydraulic doors were already open.

Inside, a man in a shirt and tie was typing at a computer terminal while a younger man waved at us from a second chair.

"He's just running the inventory system upgrades," the young man said.

The guy at the computer looked a little familiar but I could not place him.

"Oh, right, the inventory upgrade," Keisha bluffed. "They mentioned that when they sent us to condition check some of the display pieces."

At this, the older man looked up in surprise.

"You know about the inventory system upgrade?" He sounded doubtful.

"They just told us you'd be here and to stay out of your way," I said.

Then he made eye contact with me.

His hair was a different color and his posture far more confident than the last time I had seen him here, but I was sure it was the same man who had claimed to be Colin Gorman-Grey, the bumbling husband from my tour of the museum. He had none of that clumsiness about him now. He was confident and sharp-eyed.

We stared at each for a bit, then he looked over at Keisha, memorizing her face, presumably.

"You must be the new one in the department," he said to her. "I'm Gordon, from the software department."

This jerk was using the fake name I had used before!

"Felicia," Keisha said. Then she looked at me. "I guess we should get started."

We began walking back to the truck to get our gear from it.

"Don't go too far," the guy called after us. "I may need you to help me with something later."

We smiled and nodded at him, then walked as normally as we could to the back of the truck. Once we were safely behind our vehicle, all the words tumbled out of us.

"Do you know that guy?"

"I've seen him once before. I didn't know he worked here. I mean, I don't think he actually does."

"Are we burned?"

"Maybe? Yes. By him at least. But I don't know what that means."

"Should we leave?" she asked.

"Let me think," I said.

The back of our truck was filled with forged copies of art currently on display at the Lesser Museum. If anyone searched it, we wouldn't be able to explain our way out of it. Still, it seemed unlikely that this Gordon character actually worked for the museum or art handling company. If so, he would have pulled an alarm as soon as he saw us show up. And why would he have snuck into the offices back when I got my tour of the museum? The only conclusion I could reach was that he was, like me, a thief. He had been casing the joint at the same time I had been, and we had run into each other then by coincidence, and were running into each other again now by bad luck.

If I was right, he could not easily reveal who we were without revealing himself, and vice versa. The only catch was that if we got away with what he wanted to steal, he might know enough about us to tip off the authorities. We were in the same boat. Keisha could download videos and images of him from our servers if we wanted to point blame in his direction.

I explained my train of thought to Keisha.

"Have you ever come up against something like this?"

"Not really. Every once in a while, you get a sense that someone else is casing the same place you are, working the same angle, and you back off, because crowds are bad for this sort of business. But during the actual job? It's never happened to me before."

"Could we talk to him?" she asked. "See if we can split the haul with him? And I guess his team, if he has one."

"We don't know anything about him. How do we know we can trust him?"

She shrugged. "We're already trusting him, aren't we? Trusting that he hasn't called the cops and slipped out the back?"

I nodded.

There was something I appreciated about his work, as well. He had managed to get into the same administrative offices I had with seemingly far less work. He was probably a better actor than I was. Maybe he had taken an improv class with that driver I had hired.

"Let's go for it," I said. "And we'll try to parley with him at some point."

We began unloading.

TWENTY-FOUR

THEY SAY A GOOD MAGICIAN NEVER REVEALS HIS SECRETS. AND that might be true, technically. But I have found that, if you rob a magician of all their props and equipment, you can figure out how most of the tricks work. A long time ago, I had stolen such things from an aspiring young Canadian magician and took apart all his props to determine what made the illusions possible.

Don't worry! It turned out fine for the victim, as he gave up his magic act and now hosts a successful home-renovation TV show with his twin brother. And I ended up with a good supply of magic tricks, knowledge of how to rig tables with secret compartments, and a bunch of horrible glittery costumes.

The tables were useful in this job. Even though we had disabled the cameras, we did not want to do anything that looked too suspicious. Removing paintings from a wall and taking them out of their frames can cause alarm even among the laziest and most unobservant of museum guards. We had created custom workstations that we would set up in front of each work we were taking. This allowed us to take the painting down from the wall as if we were going to examine it on a special table designed just for that sort of thing. It had extra lights and swinging magnifying glasses attached to look really scientific. But that was just to distract people from the secret drawer where a copy of the painting was hidden. When we were done "condition checking" the painting, we secured it downward into the table, and simultaneously removed a copy from inside the table which we hung up on the wall in the original's place. Luckily the paintings we were stealing were all on the small side. This sort of scam is harder to pull off with large canvas works like those of the Abstract Expressionists.

To look like actual art experts, and to hide our fingerprints, we wore thin white cotton gloves. It helped that the works we targeted generally had minimalist frames which we had been able to replicate ourselves. Duplicating Old Masters is more time consuming, due to the ornate frames they are usually hung in. Even with a well-done fake of the canvas, the most casual museum goer can still spot a modern frame posing as one from a previous century. This means, to pull off a switch, you have to remove the canvas from the frame, and install your substitute, which is very time consuming. That's why most thefts of paintings from that era are just smash-and-grab jobs, even though that damages the art.

Luckily for us, the Lessaker Museum put all its faith in digital tracking technology. As long as we put the right QR code on the replacement art, they would probably not notice the switch we had made.

We got to work quickly.

The actual swaps did not take very long. The most time consuming part of the job was pretending to inspect and examine each piece of art before exchanging it for our replica. It would look too suspicious, we thought, to just take down a painting, look at it for a few seconds, then put it back up on the wall. We had to sell ourselves as art inspectors. So we walked around the artwork and Keisha typed things into her laptop.

Mostly she was confirming that the camera system was down, and then she was trying to figure out what our friend in the administrative office was up to.

Three paintings into our gambit, she let out a "huh."

"What's happening?"

"That guy left me a message."

"In the computer?"

"Sort of. He renamed a directory in the root drive. So now there's a folder called 'HelloYouTwo.'"

"Can we respond?"

"I can rename the folder to a response message, or create a folder inside it."

"Will this be traceable later?"

"No, unless he's recording his screen and our exchange the whole time. But that wouldn't hold up in court, since it could be faked. Still, we shouldn't say anything we don't want someone to have a record of later."

"Let's say, uh…" I couldn't think of an appropriate response.

"Keep it simple," she said. "I'll rename the folder 'HelloGordon.'"

"Damn. That was my fake name when I visited. You sure it won't trace back to us?"

"It shouldn't. But just in case, I'll leave Gordon out of it. I'm renaming the folder 'HelloCoworker.'"

I nodded. Then we just had to wait for a response. We moved on to the fourth and final artwork this table would hide inside. Then we'd have to return to the truck for the next magic table. We had three tables in total.

Once we had secured the new table, Keisha checked the computer again.

"He says, 'AreWeOnSameJob.'"

"No," I said. "He seems to be up to something else. Mostly in the administrative office."

"That's too long a file name for a folder."

"Sure. We should just talk to him in person. Maybe tell him we'll take a break in five, he should meet us near the truck? That way we can get out fast if we need to."

"Um. I can change the folder name 'MeetAtTruckInFive,' if that works."

"Kind of. It will depend on when he sees the message. Maybe just 'MeetUsAtTruck' but don't send it until we're heading out there?"

She nodded. We finished securing the fourth painting by Lottye Kugeios, and hung up a fake Josie had painted. Then we unlocked the wheels of the table and rolled it out towards the truck after Keisha updated the folder name.

I opened the back of the truck and we removed the second table, then carefully slotted the first table full of stolen art into its place. As we were finishing, we saw "Gordon" walking towards us slowly and calmly.

We stood with our backs to the truck, the table in front of us. He stopped on the other side of the table.

"Hello once more," he said to me.

"Good to see you again," I said.

He tipped his baseball cap towards Keisha and said, "Pleasure to meet you."

He looked at the table and then the truck.

"So I guess you're robbing the place," he said.

"If we were," Keisha said, "we wouldn't be stupid enough to say so out loud."

"Fair enough."

Nobody, including me, knew what to do next.

"The people I work for," he said eventually, "won't like it if this museum gets robbed before they want it to be robbed."

He was careful not to say *they* would be the ones robbing it, just that they wanted it robbed. I had to be similarly careful.

"I understand," I said. "But I can't really do anything

about that. If it's going to be robbed today, then it's going to be robbed today."

He thought for a while.

"I don't suppose," he said, "there's any chance we can all work together?"

I thought for a while.

"That seems unlikely."

"I figured you would say that. It's unfortunate, but I understand your position."

In the distance, we heard vehicles. Three large black SUVs appeared from behind the trees heading down the service road towards us.

"I'm going to wipe everything," Keisha said. She opened her laptop on the table and began doing whatever it is she needed to do.

"This should be interesting," the man pretending to be Gordon said.

TWENTY-FIVE

Two of the SUVs drove around us and parked right at the door of the museum. The third peeled away and parked behind us, blocking any chance of easy escape.

Large men climbed out of the cars, and looked at us. Based on bulges in their poorly tailored jackets, I would have guessed they were armed.

A smaller man with a pockmarked face, wearing a brown sweater, eased out of the backseat and slowly made his way towards our truck.

"All three of you, inside," he said. His voice had the clipped sound of a Russian accent.

I looked at Gordon, who raised his eyebrows to suggest that he did not know what was going on either. Keisha kept her cool and made eye contact with Sweater Man.

"Are you with the Foundation?" she asked him.

"I am not." He pointed towards the museum. "Inside now."

The three of us walked with our escort towards the museum. When we got there, we found the younger man from the office had been similarly wrangled by the thugs. He was in a chair facing four of the big men.

"Everyone grabs a chair," said Sweater Man, with his thick Russian accent. "Nobody to be funny."

We all sat down, the four of us now in a tidy little row in the office area.

"You are to help us taking art," Sweater Man said.

"We are professional art handlers," fake Gordon said. "Not thieves for hire."

Sweater Man back-handed him across the face, then said something in Russian. One of his henchmen pulled out a pistol and pointed it at fake Gordon.

"This is not question," Sweater Man said. "I apologize for my grammar to be confusing." He pulled out his own pistol and pointed it at Keisha.

"You think you work for Lessaker. No. You work for me." He turned the pistol toward the younger man and then towards me. "Now I ask question. You understand this?"

We all nodded slightly.

"Good. Then we have no troubles."

A phone in his pants pocket vibrated. He said something to a henchman and another man pulled a gun on us. Sweater Man put his own gun away and answered the phone.

The four of us sat in the office chairs silently while he conducted a conversation that still sounded like Russian, but I am not a language expert. For now I'll keep calling it Russian.

At first he seemed angry. He gestured to us a few times, and I was glad he had put the gun away so that he was gesturing with an empty hand. Then his anger gave way to incredulity. After a bit of this, he covered the phone and said something to one of the other men who was holding a gun. That man kind of shrugged and said something possibly rude. He and Sweater Man argued for a bit. I was certainly impressed by Sweater Man's boldness in arguing with an armed man. Finally, he spoke into the phone again, in a conciliatory manner. He rolled his eyes a bit like the person he was talking to was an idiot. And then he hung up and put his telephone away. He did not take his gun back out.

Then followed a brief conversation with his cohorts in Russian, and the other men put their guns away and walked back out towards their SUVs.

Sweater Man remained.

"There has been confusion. My men and I were to go to house, not museum." He pointed off towards the mansion. "Is house over hill, yes?"

We all nodded.

"So forget all this happen. I don't want to hear someone say something about it later. Understand?"

We all nodded again.

"I am not man to mess with. You may think about calling the law? The law cannot touch me. But I can always find you."

He walked off, and we heard the SUV doors open and close then the sounds of their engines starting and them driving away.

TWENTY-SIX

"Do you have any toilet paper?" asked fake Gordon.

"Uh. Sure. In the bathroom," said the younger man.

"Good, because I bet we all just shit ourselves, right?"

We were all afraid to stand up even though the men were gone.

"Does anybody know what that was?" I asked.

Everyone shook their heads.

"We could call the police," I said, as weakly as I could. At least three of us would be hard-pressed to explain what we had been doing here in the first place. "But he said not to," I added, "and I believe he meant it."

"Something like this happened once before," the younger man said. "It wasn't this bad, but just weird. It was earlier this year. So this might be similar? The thing was, after the last time, Mr. Lessaker's assistant came and gave us all five hundred bucks in cash to not mention it again."

"In theory, we're supposed to report any irregularities during our inspections," I said. "But I suppose we could be convinced to keep it all quiet. Money would help."

The younger man said he would get in touch with Mr. Lessaker's assistant.

"Do you all want to get back to work?" the fake Gordon asked.

"Yes," Keisha said. "Let's get back to the truck."

The three of us headed back outside.

It was calm and peaceful again. The SUVs were gone. We could hear birds chirping somewhere, maybe on the roof of the museum, or one of the cultivated trees nearby.

"I'll be completely honest," fake Gordon said. "I didn't sign up for anything like this. Just a little bit of sneaking and programming. Nobody said anything about guns and Russians. They were Russian, right?"

"I think so," I said.

"Just to get it out in the open," Keisha said, "none of us are legitimate art handlers, are we?"

Fake Gordon shook his head.

"You two are working together, I take it?"

Keisha nodded.

"Two-man team?"

"No," I said. "We have a few accomplices elsewhere. What about you?"

"I'm just freelance, I got hired by a crew."

"Maybe I know them."

"I doubt it, they're not really professionals. Well, you've met one of them, but they generally don't travel in the same circles as you, I wouldn't think."

We stood in silence for a moment.

"The security here is for shit," fake Gordon said. "It looks like you're switching out some paintings today, right? I'm setting up a camera failure for a future date. I didn't want to be here close to when my employer's robbery actually happens. I figured if I set it up far enough in advance, no one would remember me."

"Aside from the Russians, I don't think this would have been a memorable day for the museum," I said. "They shouldn't notice anything's been taken after we're gone."

He reached his hand out to shake with Keisha and then with me.

"Honor among thieves, then, right?"

We both agreed.

"I should be done in about 20 minutes," he said. "Then I'll leave you two to your work."

He walked back towards the museum.

For the next thirty minutes, we continued removing small paintings and drawings from the walls of the museum and replacing them with our fakes. Part of me wanted to flee. I don't mind other criminals, if they're polite, but I don't care for thugs. And even worse are careless strongmen. I would have understood if they had worked for Lessaker and pulled their guns to stop us from stealing. But they did not know what we were doing, or even where they were supposed to be. They just pulled their guns without provocation.

In some ways, it would make sense to leave. The museum employee would merely think we had been scared off, which would not be unrealistic. We could abandon our plan and get away with a few stolen artworks.

Leaving a job unfinished offended my sensibilities, though. On top of that, I did not like the brutes who had arrived with their weapons. Now I wanted to rob them, too, in addition to Lessaker. To teach them a lesson about resorting to violence.

I was trying to figure out how to work that angle as we finished up with the last trick table.

"We have an extra painting, Brady," Keisha said to me.

"We do?"

She pointed to a table in the truck.

"We replaced all the paintings on the target wall, and we have one left over."

"Maybe Josie messed up the count? Let's take a look at it."

Before we could do that, though, we saw a breathless man in a rumpled suit driving over the hill from the house in a golf cart, going as fast as he could, which was not fast at all.

We closed the back of the truck quickly so he wouldn't see what was in it.

The driver was not one of the Russians, I could tell right away. Then I had a premonition. The man looked familiar.

"How's my disguise?" I asked Keisha.

"It's fine. Unless someone's looking for it, they probably wouldn't notice."

"I think I know this guy," I said. "I may try to disguise my voice. Don't laugh when you hear me talk."

"I can't make that promise," Keisha said. "Even your regular voice is pretty ridiculous."

"Well, do your best."

When the golf cart pulled to a stop in front of us, the security guard from my first trip to the Museum got out and nodded at us sheepishly.

He did not seem to recognize me, but he was clearly distracted.

"Hi, I'm the director of security here and for the Lessaker household. Robert Sandover."

He stuck his hand out to shake, and we reluctantly did.

"Look, I wanted to apologize for the, uh, incident, that, I understand, happened before. There was some confusion?"

"We had a gun pulled on us!" I said in what I thought was a rough smoker's voice. Out of the corner of my eyes I saw Keisha bite her tongue to keep from laughing.

"Yes, terribly unfortunate. The Lessakers are quite wealthy and unfortunately they have some serious security situations to deal with from time to time. I'm hoping, and the Lessakers are hoping, I feel sure, that we can all put this behind us as a simple mistake."

He reached into the golf cart and retrieved two thick envelopes. I knew enough from my past work to recognize that they were stuffed full of cash.

"Is that something we can agree to?" He was still holding the envelopes, waiting for us to say yes.

"I was a bit traumatized," Keisha said. "As a woman, to have those men threaten me."

Robert seemed to consider this.

After a while, he said, "Yes, I can see how this would be difficult to forget. But we're all hoping that, with some time, we can put this behind us."

He reached into the golf cart and pulled out two more fat envelopes. He held two in one hand towards Keisha, and two in the other hand towards me.

I wanted to ask how many more envelopes he had hiding in the golf cart, but didn't want to make too much of an impression on him.

Keisha was taking the lead on this negotiation, so I looked to her. She sighed and said, "I think we can both try to forget about this whole thing." She took the envelopes from Robert and so did I.

"Well, thank you," he said. "On behalf of everyone here. And my apologies for all you've been through."

"One more thing," Keisha said, having quickly stuffed the envelopes into her back pocket. "We are supposed to report any irregularities at the workplace to our management. If we fail to do so, our jobs could be in jeopardy."

Robert's face tightened.

"So if we don't say anything about this," Keisha said, "we need to know that you won't either. You won't call the corporate office to follow up about us at all."

Robert smiled finally.

"I think you can rest assured that we will not contact anyone at your company about this."

"Then I think we're good," Keisha said.

Robert turned to me.

"I agree with her," I said, using my raspy voice again.

He nodded, then stood awkwardly for a couple of seconds and tried to look around to the front of the truck.

"Um, was there a third one of you?"

"That's Gordon," Keisha said. "He's in the administrative office." She pointed towards the museum. "He probably deserves a couple of extra envelopes—he's the one who got hit in the face."

"Thank you," Robert said, then he picked up four more envelopes and walked off towards the building.

"Is there some superstition about not counting the money while you're on a job?" Keisha asked.

"No, there's just a song about not counting your money while at a poker table. Besides, we're supposed to be terrified art handlers, not cool, calm operators. I think it would be more suspicious if we didn't look to see how much money he gave us."

We both opened the envelopes and rifled through. Each of mine had $800 in it. Keisha said hers did as well.

"First time I ever got paid *by* the people I was robbing," I said.

Once we had finished removing the art from the Lessaker Museum, Keisha took about 10 minutes wrapping up the digital part of the job. She was clearing caches, she said, to make sure there were no traces of us on the computerized security system, and then returning it to its original operating set-up so that nothing looked amiss.

As a professional courtesy, she went back into the museum to let Gordon know that she was reverting the security system to its normal functions. He told her he was finished and walked out with her to our truck.

We stood there awkwardly as Keisha typed the last few

commands into her computer to erase our footprints. Then we heard the rumbling sound and an SUV bulldozed its way over the hill on the golf cart path, tearing up the grass on both sides of the pavement before it shuddered to a stop, skidding along the lawn near us.

One of the Russian men stuck his head out the window.

"Don't be going anywhere," he said. "Not as yet."

TWENTY-SEVEN

THE RUSSIAN MAN IN THE SWEATER GOT OUT OF HIS VEHICLE less threateningly this time. He was all smiles. He even walked slowly, like a next-door neighbor coming to ask if he could borrow a shovel or rake. Of course, one usually has not been threatened at gunpoint by that next-door neighbor a few moments earlier.

"Hey, my friends," he said. "I was to hope you could help me. You are the people who move artworks, yes?"

We nodded tentatively. Was this a trap?

"My boss have some art to pack up in house." He pointed towards the mansion. "My men are … brutes, yes? Not gentle. Am told by boss to be delicate. I think, maybe these three are delicate." He gestured at us. "We could pay you, you help us with job, all cash, Mr. Sam doesn't find out."

I looked at the other two, a bit confused.

"*Uncle Sam*, he means," fake Gordon said.

"Yes, yes, Uncle Sam. The tax man! I don't tell him about our arrangement."

I looked at my watch. "How much art are we talking about?"

"Five paintings," he said. "Big ones."

"Give us a second," Keisha said.

The three of us stepped away to confer.

"I'm in," I said. "They might get angry if we say no. Plus, maybe we'll learn something useful." I was hoping to find out about these thugs so that I could rob them later as revenge for pulling a gun on me.

"Works for me," Keisha said. "I assume they're going to pay us."

"I was just in it for the one job I did, and I don't want to get hit again," Gordon said. "If you two are game, do you mind if I opt out now?"

"No, that should play. We can say your truck needs to return to the office sooner for some reason." We would have shaken hands here before he departed, but that might have looked suspicious. So we all just made meaningful eye contact before turning back towards the Russian.

"She and I can do it," I said, nodding towards Keisha. Then I pointed at fake Gordon. "But he's got to get back to the warehouse."

"My wife will kill me if we miss the flight to her family's place for Thanksgiving," he said. "Although if it was up to me, I'd definitely miss the flight. Mothers-in-law, you know?"

The Russian laughed at this. "My wife's mother was monster until I kill her," he said.

Were we supposed to laugh along with him? We did not.

"Just kidding," he added. "She is *still* monster." We smiled politely. I didn't know if he meant that she was still alive, or that he *had* killed her but she was still a monster somehow.

"Then for you two," he pointed at Keisha and me. "Drive over to house. Follow me."

"Uh, we'll head out to the road and circle around," Keisha said. "We can't risk our truck on that grass."

"Ah, the bossman's fancy truck. Yes. You know how to get to house?"

"We can find it. We just loop around that road. Someone will buzz us in?"

"Yes, gate will be open."

He hopped back into his SUV, made a tactical turn, and drove back towards the house on both sides of the small path.

"Don't get killed," fake Gordon said. "These seem like the kind of men who know how to disappear people, as they say in Ireland."

He got into his vehicle and drove away.

Keisha reopened the back of our truck and rooted through her supply bag.

"I'm going to get some tracking devices," she said. "And a disrupter so we don't leave too much of a record on any household security."

She handed me a small black plastic rectangle.

"Keep this on you. Just in case we get separated or something goes down, I'll be able to find you later."

"In whatever field they dump me in, you mean?"

"Field? They'd probably throw you into a body of water to get rid of any trace evidence. I watch enough serial killer movies to know that."

"What about you?"

"I've got one too," she said, showing me her tracking device. "I emailed the specs to Clyde. If this all goes sideways and we both disappear, he can decide whether it's worth tracking us down."

"Comforting."

She zipped her bag shut and closed the back of the truck again. "Let's hit it and quit it," she smiled. We got into the cab and she played the Funkadelic song as we drove back out into the wealthy suburban streets and towards the Lessaker Mansion.

————

THE GATES WERE STANDING WIDE OPEN, THE SUVs PARKED haphazardly in the driveway. One was way too close to the stupid, ugly fountain, and I'm sure the estate manager was having conniptions.

We parked our truck close to the end of the driveway, where we could make a fast getaway. We weren't planning to pack any art into our truck, so we didn't need to be close to the house. But Keisha pointed out that it also meant she couldn't get good access to the mansion's WiFi from the truck before we went in. I was not sure whether this was an intentional move by the Russians. If they had parked their SUVs in tight formation, we would have had room to drive closer. Perhaps the haphazard angles were strategic, because they were trained to create protective buffers with the spread of their vehicles.

Keisha threw her gear and a large thermos into a small messenger bag. I checked my disguise in the rear view mirror, and then we got out of the truck.

"Don't ask for any of my coffee," she said as we walked towards the garage.

"I've got too much adrenaline to need any caffeine," I said.

"Good, because it's a fake thermos with electronics inside it."

At the garage, they pointed us towards the front door of the house, so we went in that direction. The impressive oak door was standing wide open and we could hear Robert and the chief Russian bickering at each other. Inside the grand foyer, three large paintings were on the floor, resting against the walls where they had recently been hung. One of them had a pile of shattered glass on the floor around it, and the frame seemed a bit askew, as if it had been dropped.

In a corner of the room, we saw several large Neiman

Marcus shopping bags filled to the top with bundled stacks of $50 bills.

"Ah, the experts are here," Robert said. "As you can see, the men ran into a bit of a hiccup in trying to move the artwork themselves."

The Russian muttered something under his breath.

"The plan is to get these paintings they've purchased into their vehicles, if possible. It seems like we may have to remove them from the frames, though. Is that alright?"

"It can be bad for the paintings," I guessed. Who was going to correct me? There were no actual art experts, so as fake art experts, Keisha and I were the most knowledgeable people there.

"Taken out of their frames, the paintings are more vulnerable to tears, bending, that sort of thing. Plus they would have to be re-stretched before they could be framed and hung." I was trying to remember facts from the part of the book I had read. "And of course, the climatization process can be, uh, difficult, with unframed art."

"But you can do it?" asked the Russian.

"Sure," Keisha said. "We can roll these up to fit them in your SUVs."

Were we about to damage some classic modern paintings? I hoped not, although I supposed it would be better for us to do it carefully than to let the thugs do it, seeing as they'd already dropped one painting.

"Let me see what boss wants," the Russian said, and he pulled out a phone. He walked into another room and we could hear his footsteps echoing and most of his conversation, although we could not understand the language.

Then he popped his head back into the room, with his hand covering the mouthpiece of the phone.

"Could we just to borrow your truck, and you drive with

paintings, still in their frames, to warehouse? Then could keep the pictures in frames?"

"Depends where," Keisha said. "We have to get back to the office before the end of the day."

"Nearby," the Russian said.

"How much would we get paid?"

"Fifteen hundred each person."

He said the number so quickly I wondered if he had already discussed it with someone.

"That's on top of what we got before," Keisha said.

"Yes, we all forget about before. Is history. This is for now. Three hundreds per painting. Fifteen hundreds total."

We agreed to the deal.

TWENTY-EIGHT

SHOULD WE HAVE FELT GUILTY PRETENDING WE KNEW WHAT WE were doing? Here we were masquerading as professional art handlers, dealing with oversized canvases.

And yet, we were certainly doing a better job than the thugs had been doing before we got here. If I believed they would postpone their operation until they could find a real art handler, I would not have agreed to the gig. But it was like finding a stray dog on the street and taking it home: you might not be a veterinarian, but you're a better option than leaving the puppy on the pavement, dodging cars and likely to be struck and killed.

Part of the deception was that Keisha and I had to pretend we knew exactly what we were doing. They weren't watching us too closely, but they would notice if we stopped to check out a YouTube video about how to move a giant work of art. So we just blustered our way through and got everything loaded into our truck. We had a few extra blankets for padding but not enough to wrap all the paintings. Robert discussed the matter with a housekeeper for a while and she chose several down blankets from the bottom of a cupboard for us to take. He gave her some cash, which she hopefully pocketed herself, as I'm sure the Lessakers were not keeping track of how many blankets were in their house.

Then, wrangling some of the goons into helping us, we carried the paintings to our truck and loaded them in the back next to our tables and the art we'd taken from the museum.

"Where are we headed?" Keisha asked after we closed the truck.

"I ride with you," the Russian said. "I can give directions."

I sighed loudly.

"Listen, I understand you want to keep this secret," I said. "But this truck turns wide. It doesn't handle well." I tried to demonstrate a clumsy vehicle with my hands. "So make sure you give me a heads up in advance. No 'Turn here' at the last second like in the movies. Okay?"

"I know how to give direction," he said. I could not tell if he was amused or angry, so I did not say anything else. He got into the truck's cab on the passenger side, with Keisha in the middle between us. I did not feel comfortable asking him to sit in the small seat. He yelled some directions out the window to his men, who got into their SUVs.

"Let two of them go, then follow behind," he said. "The others behind us, yes?"

"You got it."

Luckily the driveway circled around the moronic fountain so he did not have to see me try to make a three-point turn in the truck I had only driven a few times, which might have given up the game.

At the end of the driveway, the SUVs turned right and I followed.

"It would help if they signaled," I said. "You know, turn signals?"

"He drives like woman," the Russian said to Keisha.

"That's sexist," she said. "He drives more like an old man."

"That's ageist," I said. "The last thing we want is to get pulled over for failing to signal."

"Don't keep your panties in a bundle," the Russian said. Then he took out a cell phone and made a short call in his language. "Now they will signal, just for you."

And they did. Hilariously far ahead of each turn and lane change, like they were taking a driver's test, they signaled. Sometimes they signaled a turn and then passed two or three blocks before actually making the turn. I did not mind. It was better than trying to swerve the truck at the last second.

I was busy driving, and Keisha did not seem interested in conversation, so it was left to the Russian to make small talk.

"Tell me some truth," he said, 20 minutes into the drive, as we rolled slowly down Rockville Pike. "I know these paintings are worth much money. But do you think they are so good? Pretty? Attractive paintings?"

"I don't think they're ugly," I said. "And they're not as simple as they look. However, I wouldn't pay over a million dollars for any painting, no matter how good. I guess I'm just cheap that way."

I expected him to ask me how much I *would* pay for a painting.

Instead he said, "What would you pay a million dollars for, if not painting?"

"Let me think about it," I said. I had never had a million dollars of my own. A few times after big heists, I had ended up with that much money for an hour or so, but I always had to distribute it among my colleagues. "Probably a house. You know those big ones on a cliff overlooking the ocean or a lake? And someone to take care of it for me, a groundskeeper and a cleaning woman."

"A sexy cleaning woman, right?" he asked.

Keisha laughed at this.

"What is funny?"

"He doesn't want a sexy cleaning woman," she said. "He wants someone who will actually clean. Like a … babushka?""

He grunted.

"If your maid is too pretty, she'll just sit around all day looking pretty." Keisha said. "It takes an ugly person to know how to clean."

"What about you?" I asked him. "Would you pay a million dollars for a picture?"

"Not these kind," he said, gesturing to the back of the truck. "But I one time see picture of American West. Big golden mountains, a waterfall, a few deer. Clouds reaching into sky. It took up whole wall. That is painting I would pay dearly for. It made me want to move to this country with Mr. Cesteroski."

"Albert Bierstadt," I said.

"What?"

"The painting was probably by Albert Beirstadt. He came from Germany and traveled to the West as it was being settled. He painted giant canvases and showed them like movies before movies existed. You had to buy a ticket, and then the painting was covered with a curtain so they could do a dramatic reveal for the crowd." I had spent a lot of time in front of the Biertstadt at the Smithsonian when I was younger because it was at one of the less crowded museum buildings where nobody bothered me.

"Look up 'Among the Sierra Nevadas' on your phone," I said. He took out his phone. In the crowded front seat, I knew Keisha would be able to see his security code as he entered it. He googled the title and the painting popped up on his phone. He stared at it for a while in silence.

"Is not so great on small phone," he said eventually. "Even so. I would hope to go there one day."

"The painting is in D.C.," I said. "The mountains are out in California." I did not have the heart to tell him that the landscape was probably an amalgam of a few different locations and did not represent an actual place. It didn't seem likely he would ever make it out to that part of the country, in any case.

He took out a pack of cigarettes and offered them to us. We both declined. I did not recognize the brand, and he caught me glancing at it.

"Belomorkanal," he said. "As strong as three of your Marlboros."

It looked flimsy in his hands.

"No filter, just hollow tube," he said, gesturing to the crumpled bit near his hand.

Keisha muffled a cough.

"Smells like ammonia," she said.

"That makes lungs strong," he answered, and bumped his chest with his empty hand. "Or give me cancer."

"Try not to smoke those in the same room as the paintings," I said. "The smoke will damage the canvas."

He laughed. "All artists smoke cigarette, no? I watch movies about painters, they always smoking. But I promise, I will only smoke weak cigarette near paintings, like Camel or Prima, brands with filter."

I rolled down the windows, and we drove in silence the rest of the trip, past a few big government buildings, eventually pulling into a storage space on Parklawn Drive, nestled between a used bookstore, a veterinary clinic, and an old Italian restaurant.

"Is this place climate controlled?" Keisha asked.

"Yes. Air conditioner is good."

"You need to check on humidity, too," she said. "Otherwise things will bend and crack. Make a note to check on that, or else your boss will want to move his stuff somewhere else."

"I tell him."

"When winter comes, that's when it gets bad. It gets dry and the wood will bend."

"Thank you, expert lady."

The men from the SUVs had parked neatly into the bays near the loading dock, which we backed the truck up against. It was built like a commercial storage facility, but I did not see any signs or logos. There were no digital card swipes, either, just old-fashioned locks. Inside the lobby, two big men were sitting watch. There was no desk, just men in chairs. The Russian in charge gave them a 9-digit number, which one of them checked against a list in his pocket. The guard nodded, and walked back out to the loading bay, where he undid two combination locks keeping the metal gate down, then rolled it upward like a store that was open for business.

Keisha and I supervised the henchmen as they carried the five large paintings into the building, and then to what I assume was Cesteroski's locker. There were no walls, just cages dividing each locker from the other. Some had safes inside. Others were filled with Tupperware bins. I noticed Keisha pretending to take a small sip from her thermos and wondered whether it was interacting with any digital security. We passed a cage filled with fur coats and another loaded with guitar cases. Eventually we arrived at the cage we wanted.

Luckily the door was taller than a normal household door, and we were able to walk the art right in. Keisha and I asked that the paintings be elevated from the floor and someone found some wood beams we could put underneath the frames. I tried not to look too interested in the other items in the locker with us. Most of it was in briefcases, as if it had been hustled out of a country with a courier. Probably jewelry, gold, gemstones. Maybe a few important deeds or contracts. CDs and DVDs with copies of blackmail videos and photos?

Once all the art was secure, we walked back out towards our truck. The Russian paid us.

"Forget you came to this place. If I see you around here, it will not go well."

"I sometimes shop at the bookstore down the way," I said, trying to give myself some wiggle room if I wanted to stake out the storage unit. "They have a good crime paperback section."

"Find a new place to buy books, yes?" He put his hand on my shoulder and squeezed. "At least until next year. If I see you at bookstore…" He drew a finger across his throat. "This means to cut throat, right?"

I nodded.

Keisha and I got into the truck and drove away.

TWENTY-NINE

WE WERE JUST A FEW DAYS AWAY FROM THANKSGIVING. ALONG some of the streets of Rockville, Christmas decorations were already up. Despite the scare at the end, we had finished the first part of the job. We had the under-appreciated art from the fake museum stowed in the back of our truck. The Lessaker Foundation did not know we had their paintings and did not know they now had fakes hanging on their walls. On top of that, we had gotten a pretty big cash bonus from the Russians.

A nice thing about the industrial part of Rockville and its winding roads is that it would be hard for someone to follow us without us seeing them—we could tell none of the SUVs were tailing us. Just to be safe, we parked in the loading area behind a strip mall on Rockville Pike, and Keisha swept the truck to make sure no one had placed tracking devices on it while we were occupied.

"It's all clear," she said when she was finished.

We walked around to the front of the building to eat a late lunch at a vegan Chinese place called Yuan Fu in the strip mall facing the main thoroughfare.

"I wasn't able to put any trackers on the art we put in storage," she said, after we sat down and ordered from the waiter. "They were keeping a close watch, and I didn't want to blow our cover."

"That was the smart play. Those paintings weren't the target, and we didn't want to do anything to raise our profile or get their attention at that point."

"What did we stumble into?"

"My best guess is that Lessaker sold or traded some art to a Russian gangster. Word on the street is that he's trying to hide his fortune where the government can't find it if they go after him for starting the opioid epidemic."

"*Word on the street*? Come on Brady, it's not like you heard this in a bodega near your apartment."

"Fine, I heard it from Josie. But we were eating at an outdoor restaurant when we had the conversation, so we were very close to the street at the time. Anyway, she heard Lessaker was buying art on the black market. Maybe he traded these paintings to the Russian for something else. Or sold them at a below-market rate on paper while they did some off-the-books transaction on the side."

"I think I get it," she said. "I sell you a million-dollar painting for $500,000, plus another half a million secretly in gold or crypto or something like that. When I file for bankruptcy, I've only got $500,000 in assets because only you and I know about the side deal."

"Clyde was right, you're a quick study."

"OK. I get Lessaker's angle. What's in it for the Russian?"

"I think it's a way for him to get money out of his country." I scratched my head. "It made sense when Josie explained it to me. Something about overpaying and underpaying. Or Lessaker gives the Russian paintings in exchange for money in some foreign account. Uncle Sam can't get to it, and maybe Lessaker uses that money to buy an apartment in Moscow in case he has to flee the country."

"Does any of what happened change the plan?" she said after our entrees arrived but before they were cool enough to eat.

"That's what we need to figure out."

"It doesn't seem like those Russian guys would be interested in the junk we have in our trunk."

"No, they only want big name artists," I said. "But will they get suspicious if the Lessaker Museum makes it into the newspapers for being robbed?"

"And will that somehow point back to us?"

"Hopefully not. On the other hand, if Lessaker is friendly with these goons, it could add some danger to the equation. It depends if he has enough pull with them to put them on our case after he discovers he's been robbed."

"Then I guess," she said, "we just need to make sure Lessaker and the Russians have a falling out before New Year's."

"Or just after."

"I like how you got that Russian to unlock his phone in front of me. I saw his PIN, but to be honest, I'd be too afraid to ever do anything with it. That's not a guy I'd want coming after me."

Our fake sesame chicken and faux beef with broccoli had stopped sizzling, so we began to eat.

———

I HAD BEEN IN THE BUSINESS A LONG WHILE, SO THIS WAS NOT the first time I had dealt with violent men. The trick was never to let them see your face or know who you are. Thugs are no better at solving crimes than the police are, so if you are careful to leave no traces, and have a trustworthy fence to help you unload the stolen goods, you generally have nothing to worry about.

By accident, in this case, we had stumbled into a more dangerous world than the one we intended. And Keisha and I had spent a significant amount of time with the Russian's henchman, who might therefore remember us. Even if we stole only from Lessaker, there was a chance his relationship with these Odessa gangsters was such that they would help him try to hunt us down.

———

We drove the truck north into the outskirts of Frederick, a city on the edge of Maryland's Appalachian hillbilly country, where we had arranged our own storage unit, although ours was decidedly more commercial and less full of contraband than the one we had visited with the Russians. Pretending to be vinyl record enthusiasts, we had rented a climate-controlled unit into which we now put the feminist works we had liberated from the Lessaker Museum, plus the extra painting. I would have to ask Josie about that later, but not over the phone or email.

Then we drove into West Virginia, where nobody would be surprised to find a truck stolen from a pharmaceutical company. First we parked on a small back road surrounded by trees and removed the fake art shipping company decal, revealing the old TravMG logo. We wiped down the inside of the cab and vacuumed the back, spreading all our leftover birdseed in the cargo bay, which we left open a crack. Finally, we took off our stupid disguises and switched into new ones, clothes that looked like they belonged to 9-5 working stiffs.

With all our identifiable trash stuffed in briefcases, we parked the truck in Martinsburg and caught a commuter train back into Maryland. From there, we caught the Metro subway into Washington, always sitting separately. After that, we took two separate buses back to New York. We paid for all our tickets in cash. It was close enough to the holidays that our travel was buried in a sea of other short trips by random people. Nobody would be able to track us back to West Virginia and the truck.

———

I SPENT THANKSGIVING WITH CLYDE AND KEISHA IN NEW Jersey. None of us was very much into cooking, so we got carry-out from an empanada place in Englewood. We reminisced about old jobs, but did not talk about the current one. Partly out of superstition and partly because we knew Keisha wanted it to be hers alone, to prove to Clyde she could do this without him.

Which left me in the lurch a bit, because I would normally run everything by the Old Man, just to make sure I was not missing any angles. He was a good sounding board and knew his game. Still, I resisted the urge, and after dinner took a bus back across the river to the new George Washington Bridge bus terminal in Washington Heights. I turned over the various pieces at play in my mind as I walked the empty blocks home. The only commotion was the delivery men racing in and out of the Chinese restaurants. Even the nightclub around the corner from my apartment was quiet for the evening. It was eerie, and I suddenly missed the throbbing bass line that usually kept the neighborhood awake at all hours.

In the lobby of my building, I ran into Ms. Marrillion, an old woman who lived alone on the fourth floor. She was carrying a Tupperware container full of food.

"Happy Thanksgiving, Brady," she said.

"Same to you, Willa. Did you have a good dinner?"

"I ate with Noreen in her apartment. I'm just heading home now. What about you?"

"I visited friends in New Jersey."

"You're not carrying any leftovers! Did you eat everything?"

"Pretty much."

"I'll bring you some leftover turkey and stuffing tomorrow so you can feast all weekend."

"Thank you."

I tried to keep a low profile in the building, but it was nice to know at least one friendly face. Thanksgiving is one of the only times you can truly feel alone in the city.

———

THE NEXT DAY, BLACK FRIDAY, WAS A PRIME DAY FOR ROBBERIES. Not the kind I did, but the kind where corporations steal from lower middle class bargain hunters by lying to them about sales and deals.

Ms. Marrillion woke me up at 6:00 AM to give me some Thanksgiving leftovers. After that, I took the train out to Brooklyn so I could use a public library far from my home, and I tried to find out what I could about the Russians and what sort of deal Lessaker might have made with them. A lot of the information I needed was not in print magazines, but could be found in specialized blogs about art trafficking, the Russian underworld, and money laundering.

After trying a few different incorrect spellings, I found the name the Russian had mentioned, Cesteroski, in a number of stories. Apparently he had made a fortune in selling off Soviet government assets right after the fall of communism, then turned to the oil pipeline business in the early 2000s. But when Russia began nationalizing fuel companies, he entered the organized crime world to find a more stable source of income. Now he was numbered among the oligarchs sitting atop vast empires in Russia who were trying to sneak money out for their children to enjoy the good free life of the West without arousing suspicions that they were about to bolt from the mother country.

And lately the United States was cracking down on previously reliable money laundering schemes like NYC real estate, so these gangsters were looking for new places to park their wealth. Whether in capitalism or communism, under freedom or tyranny, the rich were always trying to keep their money out of the hands of the government.

Cesteroski had also been named in several articles about questionable deaths. These tragic events were not confined to Russia, where people fell out of windows accidentally with great frequency. He'd also left a trail of bodies all throughout Europe, and, according to one paranoid blog, he was linked to a few suspicious car accidents in Virginia. He was not, it seemed, somebody one could double-cross and hope to survive. His enemies were a pile of corpses in his rear view mirror. He was ruthless.

But his men had pulled a gun on me, and I did not take that lightly.

I decided to steal his new art collection.

THIRTY

I GOT IN TOUCH WITH EVERYONE INVOLVED IN THE JOB AND LET them know where it was now heading. That way, they could back out if they did not want to go up against the Russian mob, which would be entirely reasonable

Keisha was still in. She wanted to prove herself, and besides, she was also angry that she'd had a gun pulled on her. Josie and Fiona wanted to hear the new concept first, but then, they too were in.

Much of our plan remained the same. We were still going to hit the Museum publicly at New Year's. Now we just wanted to make sure Cesteroski's men did not walk away with the Picasso, Rothko, de Kooning, or anything else.

I didn't want to steal the paintings out of the private storage unit, since the Russian goon had driven there with me and Keisha, and he would immediately be suspicious of us if that place got hit. Not that he could have easily tracked us down at that point, since he thought we worked for an art shipping company affiliated with the Lessaker Museum.

Still, it seemed more dangerous than necessary, especially

since the whole storage facility seemed to belong to criminals who would not look kindly on thieves like us.

On the bright side, it was likely that the paintings would not stay in storage for too long. If he wanted to sell them, he would transport them to another location to do so, and if he was not planning to sell them, he would hopefully put them on display in one of his residences.

We decided the best move would be to watch the storage facility, despite the Russian's warnings to stay away. This did not require round-the-clock surveillance, though. Keisha was able to piggyback onto the WiFi networks of some nearby businesses, and that allowed us to install the type of cameras people put on their front door to remotely monitor who comes knocking. They are small and cheap, and we were able to surreptitiously place them at several locations where we could watch who came and went. Mostly we were keeping an eye out for the fleet of SUVs, possibly accompanied by a van or small truck.

In any case, we were just keeping tabs. We had no plans to try to follow the fleet if it came through, since the drivers all seemed tactically well-trained and would probably notice a tail behind them.

Fiona came back into the game, making her way through high society of Washington to the Russian emigre community. After just a few days, she had a lot to tell me, so we met along the old C&O Canal and walked the towpath beside the still water heading northwest along the Potomac River. Unlike the crowded city streets of the District, the trail was a hard place to be followed. We were walking slower than joggers, and we could look in either direction and see if anyone was behind us for too long of a stretch. Nobody was.

Fiona looked like she had robbed a LuluLemon shop, decked out in high-end exercise clothes that were about to get dirty for the first time.

"It's so *lovely* to be outside on a Sunday morning," she said. "I mean, *brunch* is outside, but not *really* outside, do you know what I mean?"

"I guess," I said.

"Anyway, just to be here in nature, it's *everything*. Here, take a photo of me *before* we start walking and get sweaty. I spent half an hour getting my hair to look *decent* in a sort of hiking style. Sorry I'm late, by the way."

I took a bunch of pictures of her. She looked at them and had me take some more from a different angle, which she posted to her account.

"Won't people ask you why you were hiking and who you were hiking with?" I asked. I was worried about leaving a digital record someone could trace later.

"No, people like me will go to *marvelous* lengths to get a photo that no one else has, and hiking into the *deep* woods is simply peak content!"

Deep woods? We were only a few feet from a busy road at this point.

"And anyway, dear, it would be *more* suspicious to post nothing—people would think *something* had happened to me if I don't post my weekly brunch selfie or another pic in its place. Let's *walk*!"

We got out onto the tamped-down dirt path, among the wholesome families and exercisers, the occasional groups of high school or college kids showing off for each other, the determined dog walkers. We made small talk until we got far enough from the parking area that we weren't amid the throngs of people anymore.

"The thing that *worries* me, Brady, is how much security these people have. I think it comes from them living in a country without *any* sort of safety. They learned, you know, to take care of *themselves*. And they expect trouble to knock on their door at *any* time."

"They're paranoid?"

"They are *indeed*. That is what the last hundred years have *taught* them, you see. And they have *muscle* too. Former soldiers and gangsters who caught a ride to America to make a new start, working for them in *some capacity*, but always ready to break a few fingers if needed."

"I've dealt with tough guys in the past," I said. "The trick of it is to never give them a target. Be sneaky."

Then she filled me in on some details about Cesteroski specifically, and what she learned about his family.

"I couldn't get *too much* gossip without raising eyebrows about my weirdly specific curiosity."

"That's fine. Try to stay close to their circle, though."

Since we would not be able to follow the paintings when they left the storage facility, I was hoping Fiona could let us know if they ended up at one of Cesteroski's many homes around Washington.

We turned around and walked back to where we had parked our cars.

"*Ooh*," she said, looking at her phone. "My selfie's gotten 26 likes *already!*"

I wasn't sure what that meant, and I didn't ask.

THIRTY-ONE

THERE WAS STILL THE QUESTION OF WHAT "GORDON" HAD been doing at the museum that day. Normally I am a live-and-let-live sort of guy when it comes to other thieves. Still, I did not want his operation to interfere with mine.

Keisha did a deep computer dive but could not find any information about Colin Gorman-Grey, the name he had given back during the museum tour. And was it just a coincidence that he used a middle name Gorman, and then later called himself Gordon? Probably, since he seemed to use the name Gordon purely to remind me of my difficulty remembering the fake name I had chosen for myself. Still, it was worth keeping in mind.

What bugged me was that there was so little payoff in robbing a museum. Someone with his computer skills could make money faster in a variety of ways. So could I, for that matter. I wondered if he, too, had some ethical motivation for targeting Malcolm Lessaker. Maybe someone close to him had suffered from opioid addiction? Also, he had claimed he was a hired hand working for someone else. If that was true, what was *their* motivation? I did not have enough time to go down the rabbit hole. I would just have to hope that Colin/Gordon would not get in our way.

———

THEN THINGS STARTED HAPPENING FASTER.

First, Fiona let me know she saw a big blank wall in one of Cesteroski's apartments in the background of a TikTok video posted by one of his kids.

"I'm pretty sure I had seen *something* hanging there in a previous video. But all those *boring* videos blur together, you know?"

Was he making room to hang one of his new paintings?

Next, Keisha told me there was activity at the Russian's storage facility. Some rented vans had pulled up to the loading dock, and the drivers were the same men from the SUV caravan. Since everything else in Cesteroski's locker would have fit into a smaller vehicle, it was a good bet he was moving the art, assuming he did not have a second locker in the same building that held something bigger than what we had seen when we were inside.

So now it was a question of making sure we knew where the Russian's paintings ended up and planning a heist there that would not interfere with our plans for the Lessaker Museum on New Year's.

Everyday, Fiona would send me links to new TikTok videos from Cesteroski's children. Each was more insipid than the last. Sometimes they would give a make-up tutorial, which would be useful, I guess, if I wanted to look like a drunken toddler who got into their mother's lipstick while she was making lunch. Other times they posted "unboxing" videos, showing off luxury goods they had bought that afternoon. Watching them flaunt their wealth, I started to understand the causes of the Russian Revolution. In every video, they had their cheeks sucked in like they were impersonating starving ducks. It was almost too much to take.

But eventually I lucked out. When one of the kids attempted a viral fad called the espresso inhalation challenge, and had to run screaming from the kitchen to the bathroom to soothe his burning throat, I saw one of the paintings from the Lessaker Mansion in the living room behind his fleeing body. With that, we were in business and began making our plans.

———

FIONA DECIDED TO HOST A NEW YEAR'S PARTY. SHE FELT SHE was running the risk of being an obvious hanger-on, coasting from guest house to guest house without any place of her own to offer rich friends. Hosting a swank party would disguise her lack of fortune, because it would look like she had a lot of money to burn.

"See, Brady, when *rich* people throw a party, they waste a lot of money. They assume it's the *same* for everyone else."

"I don't like parties," I said.

"Sure, but *you're* a world-class grump. The point is, if you know what you're doing, you can actually *make* money throwing a party. You just have to devote a little time and *effort*."

She explained how she would get free products from sponsors eager to put them in the hands of influencers.

I told her it reminded me of a scam I had not been involved with but had watched a documentary about.

Her eyes lit up.

"The Fyre Festival! Yes, it will be like *that*, in that we will fleece a bunch of rich glamour boys and girls. The only difference is that my event will *actually* happen, and none of the support staff will get screwed over."

"How will it work?"

"Ah, there are a few things we *will* need to spend money on, which is why I need your help."

She did most of the hard work, finding the empty storefront of a grocery shop that had gone out of business and working out a week-long lease with the proprietor who was happy to have the space dirtied up before it was handed over to creditors who wanted to put a bank branch there. She made deals with vendors to get food and booze provided in exchange for promotion. A start-up vodka company, who advertised that their drink was carbon neutral, signed on first. Then a gluten-free caterer with an eye towards the personal chef market climbed on board. DJs are a dime a dozen, so she was able to find up-and-coming ones to fill out the whole day and night's schedule with electronic music. The party started at noon on New Year's Eve and ran through noon on New Year's Day.

Since she wasn't using the space December 27-30, she rented it out to the improv troupe that my fake driver Josh belonged to, so they could put up some of their comedy shows. I made certain I would be busy those nights so that I would not accidentally see any of their performances.

———

IN THE SECOND WEEK OF DECEMBER, TARA ELSPETH'S REVIEW of the Lessaker Museum appeared on *The Hypochondriac's* website.

The Lights Are On But Nobody's Home:

The Vapid Folly of the Drug Dealer-Funded Lessaker Museum

Who is it for?

Every museum should have a mission statement that coherently lays out its purpose and describes the audience it wishes to reach. The Lessaker Museum, paid for with the profits from Malcolm Lessaker's pharmaceutical opioid empire, lays out a lofty ambition for itself, aiming to "present the finest works of art in an artisanal setting, curated and selected with precision and taste." OK, I guess, but who's it for? Who are they presenting these works to? Not the general public, as getting into the museum is a Herculean task. It's like Fort Knox, except instead of a fortune of gold reserves, they are protecting a mediocre sampling of b-sides from some artists who deserve better than what they get here.

If you are not a friend of the Lessakers (read: rich donor), your only chance to visit the museum is by winning one of their ticket lotteries. That itself is a telling reveal—lotteries are generally a scam designed to take advantage of poor people who dream of a better life they will statistically never get. But if you're lucky enough to win a golden ticket, you must provide your own transportation into the wilds of North Potomac, Maryland, where you will jostle your way into the museum alongside a cast of characters as greedy and ill-mannered as the children in Willy Wonka's factory.

If the Lessakers truly wanted to share their art collection with the world, they could have located it near a transit hub, or made sure it was accessible via public transportation. It's ironic that such a pedestrian collection of art is not possible to visit as an actual pedestrian. They almost called the police when I showed up on a bicycle, and had nowhere for me to store it.

The building itself has all the personality of a hospital, which may be appropriate given all the prescription medicine profiteering that went into the place. Usually small museums have an advantage over the big players because their architecture can be more personalized and tailored to their collections. Regrettably, the Lessaker is built with the generic mall aesthetic and flow that afflicted The Museum of Modern

Art's 2004 incarnation, before it razed the American Folk Art Museum to feed its unquenchable thirst for more space. Hopefully the Lessaker Museum can solve its problems without demolishing any nearby landmarks. Just kidding! There are no nearby landmarks: this is a boring, affluent suburb.

As for its collection of art, the Lessaker Museum does its pieces no favors. Its outdoor sculpture garden seems to aspire towards a Storm King sort of pastoral elegance, but its garish and gaudy Versailles ambitions puncture the illusion at every turn. And someone should tell the Lessakers that outdoor works still require maintenance. Yjork Baldog's epic topiary pun *The Green Knight* (2000) looks positively malnourished, the sparse shrubbery mottled with brown patches of dying flowers. I would never argue that *The Green Knight* is a great statue to begin with, but it deserves better than to evoke images of eczema and psoriasis.

Inside is no better. The lighting seems designed to show off the lighting fixtures more than the art itself. The paintings are hung in a way that makes it impossible to see any of them without at least one major glare of a lightbulb showing up in the glass. If you told me the building had not originally been built as a museum, I would believe you, but wondered why it was not retrofitted better towards its purpose. Shockingly, though, it was purpose built to display art.

I know this reads like an art snob's hot-take clickbait, but I wasn't the only person there having a bad time. While at the museum, I talked to a man who claimed to be a student of art and museums, and he was also not enjoying his time at the Lessaker. He seemed like he was taking a test, stressed out, rather than relaxed and mesmerized by paintings and sculpture. A different man, with no interest in art, was more excited to take a tour of their offices and see their computers than he was at the chance to see the art on display. That's not a good sign.

I wanted to find one quiet corner where I could simply enjoy the work of the artists; after all, it was not their fault their pieces had ended up in this suffocating monument to one couple's ego. And yet I failed. The acoustics destroyed silence. Footsteps echoed throughout. Conversations carried. The general dissatisfaction of the people diffused into the air until a cloud of unhappiness engulfed the museum. It was no longer a cultural location. It had transformed itself into an airport terminal where all the flights were delayed. Everyone wanted to be transported somewhere, but we were stuck, with nowhere to go, wishing we had not planned this trip in the first place.

––––––

I WAS NOT AN EXPERT, BUT IT DID NOT SEEM LIKE A RAVE review.

THIRTY-TWO

MID-DECEMBER IS WHEN THE CHRISTMAS SEASON REALLY GETS going in the thieving world. Although businesses try to get started with sales after Thanksgiving, or even slightly before it, the big crowds don't turn out until those last few weeks of the year as last-minute shoppers try to cross off everyone on their lists.

Lots of luxury retail bags are placed on the floors of restaurants near Fifth Avenue. Frazzled sales people put too much jewelry on the counter to try to appease the onslaught of customers. It's easy for stuff to go missing. Everyone is distracted by the holiday lights and songs.

So it was not too hard to get the seed money Fiona needed for her big party.

Ten days before Christmas, I had drinks with my old air conditioning school co-workers. Phoebe Garlic had, in fact, moved back to Baltimore, and found work. She was in New York to close up some affairs and clean out her apartment. Byron Soop was working around town fixing heating dampers. In the city, older buildings get too hot too quickly and require multiple adjustments to try to get things to an acceptable temperature.

We headed to McManus, a bar in Chelsea. Byron didn't get free drinks there, but it was a calm oasis amidst the gentrified blocks nearby. We talked about our times at the air conditioning repair school. We caught up on what we had been doing. I did not tell them the truth, obviously, but I also did not lie.

"I got back in at the Peabody, part-time," Phoebe told us as we were finishing our first round. "It feels like home. I never quite felt at peace in New York. I was struggling all the time."

"You either make it big in this city or learn to love the struggle," Byron said. "I ain't made it big yet, so I guess I've come to terms with the daily grind."

"I think everyone in New York has made it big or dreams of making it big," I said.

"You have big dreams, Brady?"

"I do, but I can never remember them in the morning."

"What stinks about the world is that nobody's ever satisfied," Phoebe said. "A lot of companies could be fine and keep paying their employees and just exist, but some CEO tries to expand, wants to be even bigger, then runs the company out of business trying to make it grow, when it would have been fine the way it was."

"Yeah," Byron said. "People never know when enough is enough." He finished his drink and went to get us another round.

Phoebe told us about a new man she was seeing in Baltimore. She had done some internet research this time to make sure he was not a murderer.

"I learned my lesson last time. Don't fall for someone until you're sure he isn't going to kill you."

Outside the window, a bunch of idiots dressed in Santa costumes stumbled past. Somebody, years ago, had organized a bar crawl for New Jersey and Staten Island people who needed a reason to go into the city but weren't comfortable doing it on their own. So they dressed up in Santa outfits and got drunk in the afternoon, were obnoxious to everyone on the street, and convinced themselves they were cute.

Byron came back with our drinks and sat down. He told us he had started dating on the internet. It was tough, he said, at his age.

"One of the hardest parts is getting a good picture to put up. For some reason, kids know how to take good pictures of themselves these days. That wasn't a skill I learned growing up."

"Yeah," Phoebe said. "They always just had some professional take one picture of you a year at school. That was it! That was the only picture you got!"

"Maybe you got a family picture on vacation, too, but only if you had a family that could afford to take trips," I said. "And smiled around each other."

"Remember when we were young and someone got kidnapped, they only had a year-old photo to distribute?" Phoebe asked. "Kids who get abducted these days must be lucky, there's so many pictures of them floating around."

"I was thinking," Byron said, "I could make one of them, uh, selfie-sticks?" He mimed out what one was for us. "I got a telescoping inspection mirror I use to check ductwork in buildings. It's like the same length as one of those things."

"Nah, you need a trigger attached to take the pictures," Phoebe said. "A lot of the kids at the Peabody use them so I know. A real selfie-stick has a button you press to take the picture so you don't have to use the timer, which takes too long."

"Well, I don't know if I want to invest in something like that, just to try to get a date."

"It could change your life, a good photo," she said.

"I could come take pictures of you one day," I said. "Would that be weird?"

"Maybe."

"You could pose casually near the water, or on those big stairs at 187th Street."

"I'd feel silly."

"Bad news, Byron," Phoebe said. "If you find a girlfriend online, she's going to want to take a bunch of pictures of you two together. For her office, or to send to her sister-in-law, or whatever. So you better get used to posing for pictures now."

"You don't want to be that boyfriend who refuses to get his picture taken with her," I said.

"Yeah," Phoebe said. "That's what my old boyfriend, the murderer, was like. Always ducked out of photos! Don't be that guy."

We stayed until just before midnight, and then went our separate ways.

Byron was pretty drunk and I considered taking him home in a cab again and seeing if he had any blueprints for the Lessaker Museum sitting around his apartment, but I decided not to risk it. Besides, I didn't really think air conditioner schematics would affect my heist plans.

So I patted him on the back and made sure he got in a taxi safely, then walked through Chelsea.

By that point, many of the Santas were stumbling around and throwing up, having been out drinking for 12 hours. The streets were wet with melted snow, trash and leaves fluttering mildly in the breeze.

Every once and a while, a drunk Santa would be out there swaying on a corner by himself, abandoned by any friends he once had, confused about how to get back to Jersey City, or belligerently yelling at the rest of the city after being ejected from a taxi for some reason.

Luckily for obliterated Santa Clauses, a friendly man who

looked like me would help them along and get them situated at the right PATH train stop or in a car service to take them back home. When they finally woke up the next day, they might have discovered that their wallet and phone were missing. One of them even found that his selfie-stick had been stolen. (I hoped Byron would like the Christmas present I had gotten him.) These hungover Santas probably did not suspect they were robbed by that friendly man who had helped them the night before, but hopefully they learned their lesson about clogging Manhattan with their stupid antics.

ON DECEMBER 30TH, WE CLEANED OUT OUR STORAGE UNIT IN Frederick so we wouldn't have to pay for it into the next month. We loaded all the stolen paintings and boxes of pain pills into a black minivan we had rented with the driver's license and credit card of one of the drunk Santas I'd pickpocketed. Although it had been hard to tell what they looked like since they were wearing thick white beards, I had stolen from so many of them that I was able to find one who looked enough like me to fool the car rental company.

THIRTY-THREE

WE HIT CESTEROSKI'S LUXURY APARTMENT FIRST, A FEW HOURS before midnight on December 31st. His children had all gone to Fiona's party, where she was entertaining them so she could keep an eye on them.

Cesteroski and his wife went to a black-tie party thrown by a lobbyist working to lower restrictions on foreign cash coming into the United States.

They took all their personal security guards with them, leaving the place protected only by the electronic system, which was no match for Keisha. We waltzed into the building next door through the main lobby, slightly disguised, carrying a few bottles of champagne and a big bag from Glen's Garden Market. The man at the front desk did not even look up. The toughest part had been figuring out how to get the paintings out of the building without being noticed. We couldn't just walk back out through the lobby with them without being noticed and remembered.

I had considered taking them out through the service entrance, but worried the underpaid staff there would come under suspicion once the crime was discovered.

We took the elevator up to the top floor, then out onto the roof deck, where a few groups of older people were hanging out. No one saw us slip across to the Cesteroski's building next door, where we hid behind the the air conditioning unit and then snuck down into the next building.

It helped that Washington passed a law in 1910 limiting the heights of buildings to 90 meters, and developers always build to the maximum, making it easy to cross from one rooftop to another.

Then it was down to Cesteroski's apartment, which had an electronic key card entry system for Keisha to slip past. Once inside, she overrode their camera system and shut down recordings. Luckily for us, the paranoid Russian billionaire had installed his own system rather than use the services of an offsite security service who might have noticed the interruption.

"Are we just going to take the art?" Keisha asked once the electronic surveillance was down.

"We can look for his stash of cash, if you want. Jewelry and other stuff is too messy."

"Think you can find his cash before me?"

"Definitely."

"Whoever finds it first gets 75 percent. Loser gets the rest."

"Deal, but we can only look for 30 minutes if we want to stay on schedule."

And so we each took a bag and made our way through the unit. I checked the places I knew from my career's worth of experience finding things people had hidden. Keisha, meanwhile, examined where the cameras were and tried to locate a safe based on which parts of the apartment were most under scrutiny.

I started in the office. Next I'd try the bedroom, but I assumed he would keep his money somewhere his wife would not come across it by accident.

Keisha went to the bedroom closet first.

After a few minutes, I heard her yell "Bingo!"

I kept rifling through his office.

It was boring. He wasn't the kind of guy to keep actual files in there. I doubted he even kept records of most of his business, which was probably all off the books, handled in vague threats over phone calls or in person at public locations to prevent being recorded. It looked like an office in a furniture catalogue. No loose pieces of paper, no drawer overflowing with receipts.

Still, I felt this would be the place. I eliminated the desk pretty quickly. It was modern, without a lot of drawers or places things could be hidden. Then I turned to the bookshelf along the wall. It seemed more decorative than functional. A bunch of leather-bound classics he had bought as a set or been gifted. Not a single crime, fantasy, horror, or romance novel, which is always a sign that it's not a real reader's bookshelf.

I looked for something that stood out—not a single book, which would be too obvious, but a cluster of books. I began pulling on each volume slightly to make sure it moved and eventually found the books that were connected to each other. It was a three-volume set of Robert Burton's *Anatomy of Melancholy*. They seemed authentic, so someone had custom-made this cache. Inside were stacks of cash, mostly American dollars, but also bundles of rubles, Euros, and yen. I crammed it all in my bag, then put the empty books back on the shelf and went into the bedroom where I found Keisha.

"Five thousand bucks," she said, pointing to her small stack of cash on the bed.

"That must have been the wife's private stash," I said, dumping my haul onto the bed next to it. "Here's *his* contribution to our cause." It was a couple hundred thousand in U.S. dollars. I didn't bother trying to estimate the foreign currency.

We spent a few minutes stowing the cash into our bags, then moved on to our main task.

Inside our gourmet food bags, we had digital reprints of the paintings we were going to steal. Any expert would spot the difference in a second, but we figured it would take the Cesteroski family a few days to notice that their paintings no longer had brush strokes, depth, or dimension; that they had suddenly gone flat.

When the numerous pizzas we had ordered digitally with a fake account arrived at the front lobby, we took advantage of the distraction to get the five original paintings up onto the roof. I admit that exposing them to the environment was the not the best way to treat them, but I could not think of any other way.

A few buildings down, near where we had parked, was an ugly modern glass condominium. To keep its facade sparkling and clean, that building had a specialized cleaning platform that could be lowered from the top of the building. After carrying the paintings over, we used that lift to get the paintings back down to ground level.

We loaded them into our rented van along with the cash, and I took a set of fake frames back up on the lift while Keisha drove to a parking lot to make sure there were not electronic trackers on any of the paintings or money.

I crept into Cesteroski's apartment one last time and assembled the frames to hang our replacement paintings. If his family was as shallow and oblivious as we thought, they would not notice for some time.

Then I exited up to the roof, back across to the building we had first come into, and mixed in with the guests on the rooftop deck. I dumped the old gourmet food bags into the trash and left the bottle of champagne for one of the guests there.

I took the Metro out of the city and into the Maryland suburbs, where Keisha picked me up in the van.

Then both of us dressed up in tactical gear to rob the Lessaker Museum.

THIRTY-FOUR

We knew nobody was home in the giant Lessaker Mansion. Malcolm and his wife had gone to a party thrown by a once-famous law professor who now specialized in defending wealthy sexual harassers. (He was making a fortune because there were so many of them.)

And as a holiday bonus, the Lessaker house staff had all been gifted a weekend at a spa near the shore, so they were out of the picture too. It was off-season at the shore, so that gift was not as generous as it sounded. And the museum was hardly ever open to start with, so none of its staff would be working there on a holiday.

We parked near the service entrance to the museum and Keisha opened it for us with some sort of device.

"This isn't even that secure," she said. "What I did was basically like trying a bunch of garage door clickers until the right one opens it."

We pulled up masks over our faces and drove in, along the trees, towards the museum building. In the dark, with all but the security lights off, it looked like a scale model of a shopping mall from the early 1990s.

Keisha got out her laptop.

"I'm going to make sure all the cameras are off before we get out of the van."

I played with my gloves while I waited.

"Huh," she said.

"What?"

"I said, 'Huh.'"

"What does 'huh' mean?"

"It means *I don't know*," she said. "If I meant something specific, I'd have said an actual word. Something's up though."

"Huh."

"It looks like everything's already down. The whole system."

"You got it down that fast?"

"No, it was down when we got here."

"That's weird. Second time that's happened to us."

"Yes, it is."

"Maybe the museum doesn't keep it on all the time?" I asked out loud. Then I frowned, although she couldn't see it because of my mask. So I shook my head back and forth. "That seems unlikely."

"The issue is that without knowing why it's down, I can't be sure it will stay down," she said. "Like the whole thing could just be rebooting, and it may come back online in a bit."

"Should we wait?"

"What if it's not rebooting? Then we'd be sitting here all night."

"Well," I said. "Let's not look a gift horse in the mouth. The mouth being a security camera in this case."

"Let me tell you what. I'll set up a ping every 15 seconds. If it starts to come back online, I'll get a notification and we can take it from there."

"Sounds good," I said.

She typed a bit more to set up this system she'd devised.

"Good to go."

She folded up her laptop and stowed it in her small backpack.

"I'm putting the key in the ashtray," I said.

"Gotcha."

In case one of us had to leave without the other, the key needed to stay with the van. But leaving it in the ignition would make it easy for police or a security guard to find and remove. Hopefully none of that would matter.

We got out of the van and walked toward the museum.

————

GETTING INSIDE WAS EASY, AND WE DID NOT NEED TO CAREFULLY remove the paintings, since we knew they were the fakes we had installed a month ago. We turned on our flashlights and made our way to the gallery. It would be easier to work with the museum lights on, but that could have caused a neighbor to notice and report it to someone.

"I guess we have to switch to headlamps now," I said.

"This is the nerdiest thing I have ever done," Keisha said.

We put away our flashlights and turned on the headlamps we had bought from a camping store.

"I'll start on the left, you start on the right," I said.

I thought I heard her say something in response, but couldn't make it out.

"What?"

"I didn't say anything."

"I thought you said something."

"No, I didn't," she said "Hey there's something weird here. Like paint?"

Then I heard a buzzing noise.

"My program's pinging me," she said.

Then all the museum lights turned on.

It is not easy to explain why you are in a museum after hours dressed in tactical gear and a face mask. I tried to think of an explanation in case we did not make it back to the truck before we were noticed.

And then five sexy dinosaurs entered the gallery space holding rifles.

———

"DON'T MOVE," SAID THE DINOSAUR CLOSEST TO US.

"We won't," Keisha said.

At that point, I saw the paint on the wall Keisha had mentioned before. It was a long sentence spray painted across the whole gallery, winding its way around the framed pictures. I did not have time to read the whole thing, but it seemed like a manifesto. Mostly because it was too long to just say something pithy like "your mom sucks" or "eddie was here" or "#graffiti."

"Are they cops?" asked one of the dinosaurs.

"Nah, I don't think so," said the dinosaur closest to us, who I assumed was the leader, because she was a Tyrannosaurus rex.

Earlier when I said they were sexy dinosaurs, I did not mean to imply that prehistoric, extinct reptiles are erotic to me. I should specify that these were actually women in bikinis with dinosaur masks covering their faces.

"These two look like robbers," the T. rex said, leveling her rifle at me.

"Is that a pellet gun?" Keisha said.

"What?" I said.

"Shut up. We're asking the questions," the T. rex said, turning her rifle towards Keisha.

"It is! That's a pellet gun!"

"Well, it will still hurt," the T. rex said.

"Have we met before?" I asked. The dinosaur's voice was familiar.

"I don't know, I can't see your face," the dinosaur said to me. "You're wearing a mask."

"So are you."

"Good, glad to get that squared away. By the way, I'm not really a dinosaur."

"They've never even heard of us!" said a Triceratops, dejectedly. "After all we've done."

"I told you, this job was going to be the one that put us on the map," answered the T. rex.

"Are you robbing this museum too?" I asked.

"It's not really a museum," the T. rex said. "It's a fascist trophy room."

"Tara?"

"Oh shit," the T. rex said. Then she cocked her scaly head at me. "Gordon?"

"This dinosaur is the art reviewer?" Keisha asked.

"Yes, but we're not thieves like you two," Tara the T. rex said. "We aren't stealing anything. Just bringing attention to the poor security of this private collection. We're hoping to get their non-profit status revoked." She gestured at the pictures on the wall. "These paintings are not in safe hands."

"And," I said, "they're fakes."

Tara removed her T. rex mask and looked closely at the paintings. "Well, shoot."

After that, Keisha and I had a long conversation with the gang of dinosaurs.

THIRTY-FIVE

"WE'RE AN ACTION GROUP CALLED DINOSAURS FOR THE Accessibility of Museums by People. We're kind of new on the scene," Tara said. "The Guerilla Girls focus on gender and ethnic representation in the art world. We are focused on the role of money and finance in the art world. It's become a tax shelter for millionaires and billionaires to park their fortunes. None of them care about art. We want to bring the public's attention to the situation."

I did not know who the Guerilla Girls were, but it did not seem like the time to ask.

"You're Dinosaurs for the Accessibility of Museums by People?" Keisha asked. "Wouldn't that make you D.A.M.P. for short?"

"We're not very good at acronyms," sighed the pterodactyl.

"We filmed our adventure in the museum and we're going to take over the Lessaker's website to host the video," Tara said. "We want to show the world that this place is a joke. It's a private collection, not a museum."

I explained to her what my plan with Keisha had been.

"I figured you were up to something when Andy told me you snuck in during Thanksgiving dressed as art handlers."

She gathered all of D.A.M.P. for a brainstorming session. Tara did not want it to look like her group had replaced all the paintings on the wall with forgeries. And for their safety, I did not want them caught up in my caper with the Russians either.

So, since Keisha and I had the originals in the minivan, we rehung them in the museum, undoing our earlier heist. It took us about ten minutes. We discovered the extra painting, again, and I realized I had forgotten to ask Josie about it. While we replaced the forgeries with the real things, the dinosaurs continued spray painting their manifesto all over the museum, careful not to deface any of the actual art.

I'll admit, it wasn't every day that I broke into a place to return something I had previously stolen.

The way I figured it now, someone from the museum would be forced to call the police and insurance companies when they saw what the Dinosaurs for the Accessibility of Museums by People had done. That was something we could work with.

Still, we had not stolen much we could make a profit off of, which meant I'd be losing money this year if I did not figure out another solution. We had the cash the Russians had paid us back before Thanksgiving, plus what I'd taken from the Santa Clauses, and the money we'd gotten from Cesteroski's apartment. The art we stole from Cesteroski was also still in the van, but I didn't plan to sell any of it.

I told Keisha that it was looking like we might lose money.

"We could see what's in the vault," Keisha said

"What vault?"

"He's got a secret vault off the admin office of the museum."

Tara and I looked at each other.

"They didn't show us that on the tour," I said.

"That's because it's a secret vault," Keisha said. "But I compared the registered blueprints with the finished building and there's some space missing."

I suddenly felt stupid for not getting air conditioning schematics from Byron, which might have shown me the same thing, but did not admit it to anyone.

"And," she said, "I also went through the museum's bank accounts and found payment to a company that makes custom safes just before they opened. So there's definitely a hidden vault."

She was certainly thorough! I made a note to tell Clyde how well she'd done, although I'd probably let him think I had also discovered the vault independently of her research.

"Well, sure, let's check it out," I said.

"Count on the rich to be sneaky turds," Tara said.

———

KEISHA OPENED THE HYDRAULIC DOORS WITH HER COMPUTER and led us back into the administrative offices, which were still dark. We turned our headlamps on, but then Tara flipped on a light switch for the whole room.

"Are you worried about neighbors reporting the lights on?"

"Nobody's home at any of the surrounding houses," she said. "We checked. Besides, the Lessakers often come back to the museum when it's not open and use it for lounge and party space. They consider it another wing of their house. So nobody will suspect anything if they see the lights on."

Keisha directed us to a bookshelf.

"Does this seem out of place to you?" she asked.

"Well, now that you mention it, yes," I said.

"Everything else in this place is custom-built and matches the sterile white look," Keisha said. "Then there's this flimsy brown bookshelf you could buy at a box store."

"Not a lot of books on it, either."

Keisha leaned into it with her shoulder and it moved a few feet. She shoved again and it cleared an opening on the wall behind it. She used her leg and kicked it the remaining few feet so we could see the hidden doorway. There was a large vault door.

"Is one of you a safe cracker?" Tara asked.

"He is, or so I've heard," Keisha said, pointing at me.

"I am, but you don't need me for this," I said. "It's not locked."

"Why would he buy an expensive safe but not keep it locked?"

"He's lazy. Probably forgot the combination a few times and hated calling the safe company. Plus, he thinks it's well hidden. But just for the record, and my own pride, I could have opened it if I had to."

Keisha swung the door open and we looked inside. The big Neiman Marcus shopping bags full of cash we had seen at Thanksgiving were inside. So were a bunch of boxes of documents and some hard drives.

"Fifty-fifty split on the money, Tara?"

"Sure, Gordon. Just so you know, we're not going to keep it for ourselves. We'll use it to fund future projects like this."

"We'll be spending ours," I said. "We're just common thieves. I trust your people to split it, while we look at the rest of the stuff in there."

She assigned some dinosaurs to the task of divvying up the cash. We pulled out the boxes and hard drives. Tara and I rifled through the paper files while Keisha pulled out her laptop and scanned through the hard drives. It only took us a few minutes or so to get the gist.

"These are all records of Lessaker's TravMG drug trials and how they knew their stuff was addictive," Keisha.

"Yeah, that's what we found, too," I said, holding up some

of the papers. "Internal warnings, concerns, and stuff like that."

"Why would Lessaker keep all this?" Tara asked. "It seems like it incriminates him."

"Insurance," Keisha said. "It incriminates him, but it also incriminates the other companies and players. None of them can throw the others under the bus this way. They're all in it together."

"He really should have kept that safe locked," I said.

"I thought you said you could have opened it," Keisha laughed.

"Definitely I could have. Probably. I think."

The dinosaurs had finished with the stacks of cash.

"Assuming these bundles are all the same amount, it's all split except there's an odd number and this one's left over," said the Triceratops, holding up a brick of cash.

"You can have that one," I said.

"We should check them for transponders," Keisha said.

"You can do that?" Tara asked.

"Most definitely," she said. She took some contraption out of her sling bag and plugged it into her laptop, then ran it up and down all the stacks of cash. Nothing beeped, and it seemed like nothing concerning popped up on her laptop. "All set. But just to be safe, I'd remove these bands and throw them away as soon as possible. Go through each stack looking for anything hidden inside. Even if it's not a tracker, it can identify the money later and you don't want to be caught with stolen money."

"Do you want these files?" Tara asked.

"I wouldn't mind having them."

"I'd take them, but we have nowhere safe to store them currently. And they'll point back to this job."

"We'll put them in our truck. We have to unload some stuff anyway."

Keisha and I toted our portion of the cash and the all incriminating documents out to the minivan. Then we removed all five paintings we'd taken from Cesteroski's apartment and stowed them inside the secret vault in the museum office. I had originally planned to put them in the Lessaker Mansion, but this seemed to make more sense. We also planted the pills we'd stolen in New Hampshire inside the vault, along with all the money, both dollars and foreign currency, that we'd taken from Cesteroski's place. It pained me to leave any money behind, but I figured it would keep the Russian from looking for someone besides Lessaker when he found out he'd been robbed. That would keep us and the dinosaurs safe, hopefully. Besides, we had all the cash from the shopping bags

"Do we need to wipe the security logs or anything?" I asked.

"I doubt it," she said, "but I'll take a look."

"We spray painted over the lenses of all the cameras before you arrived," Tara said. "And the virus Andy put in their system back on Thanksgiving will erase all the data at 6:00 AM this morning. We should be clear."

"Looks good to me," Keisha said, reading something on her laptop. I think she was looking at the database, but I don't really know how any of that works.

We closed the safe and put the bookcase back in place.

"Alright dinosaurs," Tara said, "let's make ourselves extinct."

I tried to think up something clever to say as well, but didn't have any ideas.

"Time for us to steal away, too" I said to Keisha, who groaned.

"Maybe you should sign up for one of those improv courses, Brady."

"I'd let the Russians kill me first," I said.

THIRTY-SIX

THERE'S A SCENE IN ALL THE HEIST MOVIES WHERE THE TEAM gets together at the end to distribute the loot and celebrate, usually in some sort of warehouse. But it's never like that in real life. Gathering everyone in the same place is dangerous. If the authorities are on anyone's trail, they will soon discover all the players involved. So we kept our distance and covered our tracks.

We stowed the fake paintings in the ArtLocatr office at the co-working space in D.C., then returned the rented minivan. Keisha took half of our cash with her back to New Jersey. I bought a ticket on an anonymous Chinatown bus and took the rest of the cash back to Manhattan. I tried my best to look hungover on the bus, to blend in with all the other partiers making their way back north on January 1st.

If all went according to plan, Cesteroski would think Lessaker had double-crossed him and stolen back the art he had sold the Russian in November.

A few days later, a big snowstorm hit the East Coast, burying Washington and New York. So I had a lot of time to sit inside and read the newspapers.

First, there was a story about the Dinosaurs for Accessibility of Museums by People video, which went online January 2nd, on the Lessaker Museum website, which had been hacked. D.A.M.P. was not taken as seriously as Tara would have liked, I think. The newspaper implied that they were dilettantes with too much time on their hands. Sure, the article seemed to suggest, anyone with evil intent and disregard for the law could break into a museum and cover it in graffiti, but what did that prove?

The next day was different, though. At first it was an exclusive in *The Washington Post*. The insurance investigators called in by the Lessaker Museum to deal with the D.A.M.P. vandalism had noticed some irregularities in the artwork and brought in an expert to authenticate the paintings in the collection. It was discovered that one was a forgery.

Once there was blood in the water, the other journalists dived in and the feeding frenzy began. A New York tabloid talked to a Maryland police detective who reported an unusual discovery within the museum itself which he could not discuss further. An investigative magazine posted a story to its website revealing that a legion of art experts had been called in to explore some oddities within the museum.

Attempts to track down Dinosaurs for the Accessibility of Museums by People were unsuccessful, and the police complained frequently to journalists that the security system at the Lessaker was a mess, with hours, if not entire days, of footage missing along with the data logs.

The Lessakers returned from their travels a week into the new year, and gave a number of interviews asking, *who would do such a thing to a museum?* They declined to comment on the question of forgeries or other irregularities in the museum. At this point, they were only allowed into their home. The state's attorney had closed off the museum as a crime scene.

A few days later, it was reported that the Lessakers were

denied in their attempt to board a flight to Vietnam from Dulles airport. A young social media influencer recognized them and filmed them being rejected. "We can't even go on vacation?!?!" yelled Malcolm Lessaker as he dragged his giant suitcase through the airport back towards the parking lot. Most local news channels reported on it, perhaps because it had good video, and they noted that Vietnam does not have an extradition treaty with the United States, which may have been why Lessaker was headed there

Finally the big story broke two weeks into January, in the Washington paper's Sunday edition. There was a big color photo, on the front page, of two FBI agents standing in front of the secret vault in the museum's administrative offices. Arrayed in front of them were the several large stacks of cash, several boxes of pills, and the paintings we had stolen from Cesteroski's apartment. The headline shouted **ART, MONEY, LIES: Inside the Secret World of a Billionaire's Museum**.

The story detailed how an investigation into a vandalism incident led to the discovery of a secret vault inside the museum.

It started with a prank.

On New Year's Eve, a group of still unidentified women videotaped themselves defacing the walls of the Lessaker Museum in North Potomac, Maryland. According to their manifesto, they were protesting "the private collection of art posing as a public one in order to avoid paying taxes."

Art, according to the group calling itself Dinosaurs for Accessibility of Museums by People, should belong to the people.

Police and insurance investigators were working together on the case of the break-in, according to a high-ranking detective with the Maryland State Police, when a tip led them to a secret panel behind a bookcase in the museum's administrative offices.

At first, it seemed only to be a secret storage unit, not completely out of the question in the case of a museum with highly valued paintings in its collection.

However, the investigators discovered that paintings inside the vault were part of Malcolm Lessaker's private collection, which would be a violation of the museum's non-profit charter.

A spokesman for Mr. Lessaker said that the paintings were most likely gifted to the museum's collection by the generous Lessaker family and the paperwork would turn up shortly.

But that wasn't the only secret.

Treasury officials were called in due to a large amount of U.S. dollars and foreign currency found hidden inside, according to an official who chose to remain anonymous, due to the fact that they are not authorized to speak about pending investigations.

And several neighbors reported the presence of Drug Enforcement Agency investigators among the scrum of law enforcement officials.

"Yeah, there were a whole bunch. I remember because of all the windbreakers with the letters. FBI, DEA, ATF, Treasury," said Terrence Connor Fritz. "I was riding by on my 1967 Triumph T120 TT Special, and I got scared for a second that they were arresting me for having too cool a motorcycle." He laughed. "Just kidding. It ain't a crime to be cool, as far as I know."

Some pharmaceutical grade opiates that had previously been reported stolen from a Lessaker-owned manufacturer in New Hampshire were also found in the vault according to a high ranking officer in the DEA who asked to remain

anonymous as they were not authorized to speak publicly on
the investigation.

"Someone had deactivated the RFID chips to try to cover
their tracks, but we were able to reactivate them," the DEA
officer said.

The story went on for a while about what had been discovered so far, but as of yet, no agency had released any official
statement.

The next few days saw follow-up stories with more anonymous sources adding an extra detail here or there. Cesteroski
never came forward to mention that he had purchased the
paintings from Lessaker and they had been stolen back from
him. Nor did he attempt to claim any of the other things stolen
from his apartment. In fact, he stayed out of the press
altogether.

Then Lessaker gave a bizarre news conference outside his
home, in the big driveway with the useless fountain where I
had first met Tara.

It did not air live on television, but I was able to find it
online later. Well, Keisha was able to find it online, and she
sent me a link.

Lessaker had a lawyer on one side and a couple of big
security guards hovering close by. They were the kind who
probably used to play football, or were bodybuilders. Big and
intimidating looking, but not terribly skilled when it came to
fighting or outwitting the enemy. You wouldn't pick a fight with
these guys in a bar … and you could expect to find them in a
bar pretty frequently, doing shots and saying crude things to
women. If you were criminally minded, you could steal their
cars while they were drinking. Generally, when you hire a
bodyguard, you want somebody alert, and these guys had
never paid attention a day in their lives, except maybe when

someone explained to them how to beat a steroid test. But they looked scary, if nothing else.

"My client would like to address the rumors and hearsay that have been irresponsibly leaked to the press, seemingly by law enforcement, if we are to believe the newspapers," said the lawyer, with a sneer that implied he did not trust the media. "I should like to add, before he begins, that the United States of America guarantees its citizens the right to a fair trial, in a court of law, not on tabloids and Twitter. So let's call off the witch hunt. Let's put away the pitchforks and tiki torches and stop burning books until my client has his day in court."

With his mixed metaphors, it was not clear to me whether he believed his client was an innocent schoolgirl in Salem, a dude-bro on vacation in Hawaii, or Frankenstein's monster.

Then Lessaker spoke into the bouquet of microphones with news logos on them.

"Hello. I am Malcolm Lessaker. My wife and I are collectors of art. We built this museum," he gestured off into the distance, "to share our love of art with the public. It was a gesture of love. And of goodwill. We wanted to build something ... for ... the community."

Here he pretended to get choked up, but not very well. Maybe *he* should have signed up for an improv class with my fake chauffeur. Lessaker's lawyer handed him a handkerchief that was too readily available. The crying had clearly been planned in advance. Lessaker brushed at the part of his face where tears would have been.

"Now we are being maligned. We are being gossiped. People are saying things about us. Well, I'm here today to say that none of it is true. Nothing anyone says about us has ever been true. We are not the elite. We are not tax cheats. No one is doing anything, from my level on down, that is immoral, illegal, inappropriate, or anything else. I'm not the king of England. I haven't exploited foreign workers on my domestic staff. I did not make a fortune of blood money off America's addictions." The lawyer whispered in his ear, and Lessaker made air quotes with his fingers. "Quote unquote. Those last couple things I said were quotes." The lawyer sighed and frowned.

Lessaker continued, with a message that was probably intended for Cesteroski:

"I want to say, to anyone who is listening, that we have been framed. I do not know why, but a lot of the things we're being accused of aren't even true."

He pointed at the assembled cameras.

"You so-called journalists write them in the way you want to present them, instead of in reality. You are completely misrepresenting situations. You have placed me and my family in harm's way and it is unacceptable. So, like, what's even going on? I did not steal any paintings. I can't make that clear enough. I was out of town, and I don't know how those paintings ended up in my museum." The lawyer nudged him. "Not *my* museum, of course. I meant *the* museum. The museum that belongs to the public. I just ... I trust that the paintings will end up back in the hands of their rightful owners, and we can just ... listen, we can figure this out. I am a family man. My wife wishes she could have been here with me today, but she has chosen not to. At this time I will take a few questions."

"We will not be taking any questions," the lawyer said, and he hustled Lessaker away with the bodyguards.

The reporters shouted questions at him as he disappeared into his high-class garage.

———

BY THE END OF JANUARY, A FEDERAL PROBE HAD OPENED. ITS specific target was money laundering, narcotics distribution, and tax evasion, but the government attorneys had broad scope to investigate additional crimes they uncovered during the course of the investigation.

By that time, Keisha had been able to make copies of all the documents we had taken from Lessaker's vault. She delivered the originals to the press anonymously.

They had a field day exposing the shady back-room dealings that had allowed Lessaker to make billions off of his addictive pain-killing medicine.

He scheduled another press conference on his driveway, to "clear up the misinformation and lies" that the media had been reporting about him.

There were a lot more reporters for the second press conference. This one I was able to watch live on the news. It started 45 minutes late. There were a number of police cars parked on the driveway. The lawyer came out, along with the chief of Maryland police, and a man who identified himself as an FBI agent. He spoke first.

"Malcolm Lessaker is missing, and if anyone has information about his whereabouts, we ask that they contact us immediately. His wife is missing, too."

The reporters immediately started shouting questions. The lawyer said that he had no idea where Lessaker or his wife were, but that he was worried about them.

The Maryland police chief gave out the phone number for a tip line and a website. They released a photograph of one of Lessaker's cars, the green Jaguar convertible, which was also missing.

They took a few questions. The gist of it was that they did not believe Lessaker had fled willingly, and they were treating the couple's disappearance as a missing persons case.

THIRTY-SEVEN

MALCOLM LESSAKER WAS NEVER SEEN AGAIN. AT LEAST NOT BY anyone who reported it.

His mansion burned down on Valentine's Day. The authorities said it was a case of arson, the fire having been ignited by a number of simultaneous Molotov cocktails thrown through the windows, and accelerated by gasoline spread throughout the house beforehand.

A month later, Lessaker's green Jaguar was found abandoned in the woods in rural West Virginia. It's possible that he and his wife drove their car into their woods, then vanished into a new life, which would account for the second set of tire tracks found nearby. But that seems unlikely. More probable is the theory that the Lessakers were driven into the woods in their own car, then killed and buried there. In addition to finding a shovel nearby, police reported the curious fact that the ashtray of the Jaguar was full of Russian cigarette butts, specifically the Belomorkanal brand.

I still remembered what Cesteroski's henchman had said to me the first time we met: *I am not man to mess with. You may think about calling the law? The law cannot touch me. But I can always find you.*

———

THE LESSER MUSEUM'S NON-PROFIT CHARTER WAS REVOKED and most of its collection was absorbed into the Smithsonian's holdings. A few pieces, by artists already well-represented in the Smithsonian collection, were auctioned off, and the money donated to fund research on opioid addiction. Still, despite the goodwill that generated, an attempted exhibit of the recent Lessaker acquisitions at the Hirshhorn Museum and Sculpture Garden met with such outcry that it never happened.

I was a little disappointed, as I had hoped the Dinosaurs for the Accessibility of Museums by People might show up there.

Instead, the next time I heard about them was in New York, where they organized an art appreciation day to escort underserved children from around the city into normally stuffy art galleries and museums to try to make the spaces less intimidating. For that project, they abandoned the dinosaur costumes and dressed like popular superheroes that children enjoy.

They were now calling themselves Heroes for the Utilization of Museums by People, which I guess made them H.U.M.P.

They still weren't very good at acronyms.

Lawyers attempting to wind up the estate of the missing (and presumed dead) Lessakers ran into trouble because the couple had left everything to their non-profit, which no longer existed. Since their parents were long deceased and they had no children, the executors of their will had to work extra hard to locate their next of kin. Eventually, through the magic of DNA and ancestry websites, they were able to find an offspring of Malcolm's grandmother, Lizzy Lessaker, née Humboldt. Remember her?

Morris Humboldt, the child she had given up for adoption in exchange for entry into the Lessaker clan, had survived despite all the odds. His oldest grandson, Jose Guzman-Woods, was an immigration lawyer in Brooklyn. There wasn't too much money left after the government took their share, but Guzman-Woods inherited enough to fund a life of pro-bono work.

At the beginning of summer, Fiona the Grifter decamped from her Washington, D.C., guesthouse and bought a small home on Hydra, an island in Greece. She got some money from our heist, but most of what she paid for it was the profit from her New Year's party, which had been a huge financial success.

———

I visited Josie in New England in June. It was easy to blend into the crowd of visiting parents during graduation festivities at the college, so I was not worried about us being connected, and I was pretty sure nobody was looking for anyone involved in the Lessaker Museum heist anymore.

We got dinner at The Jewel of India restaurant in Hanover, New Hampshire. The weather was nice enough for us to sit out on their back patio. Our conversation ended the way it often did when we weren't talking about a job. I tried to convince her to move to New York, while she tried to get me to retire and settle down, maybe move to Vermont and live with her.

"Do you ever think it might be nice to give up your heists and just relax, take things easy? Not look over your shoulder all the time?"

"I'm the restless type. I can't sit around the house all day."

"You could get a regular job, Brady. Lots of people do it."

"I think I'd get bored."

"For kicks, you could sneak out at night and make renegade

improvements to the neighborhood. Fix someone's gutter without them knowing. Repair the playground equipment at the park in secret. Stuff like that."

"Or you could move to New York."

"Ahh, yes." She smiled unconvincingly. "You know I got an offer for a four-days-a-week job at Columbia. I would start with the new school year."

Hope bloomed within me, but I tried to sound indifferent.

"You should take it. I think you'd like being back in the city."

She smiled. "I do have the number for a ramen place in SoHo we could try. But I can't be in the same town as you while you're still doing what you do, Brady. I would always run the risk of getting sucked in. I had to move all the way up here just to get away, and you still found me and brought me into your schemes."

"I guess I'm just charming that way."

"Forgery is one thing," she said, "but stealing is another."

She poked at the remains of a samosa with her fork.

"I have something here," she said. "A kind of home. It's not what I dreamed of, but it's something. If I thought I could have something like this in the city, I would move."

I thought about it. We had never had a big moment, an ultimatum. We had just chosen different paths in life and drifted apart. But I guess we were the question marks hanging over each other's lives. What if we had made different choices? Could we have stayed together? Were we too old to change for each other?

"You told me you had a regular job for a while, didn't you?" she asked. "Managing classes at an air conditioning repair school or something like that."

"Apparently, a couple of decades of planning heists gave me a good eye for detail and getting things done."

"But you left to start stealing again?"

"Only because I had to. The owner had been treating the tuition revenue like his personal bank account and one day we just ran out of money."

"Do you think you could go back to something like that?"

I shrugged. I honestly was not sure. "I didn't realize I missed my old life until I fell back into it," I said. "Now I don't know if I'd be happy behind a desk."

After dinner, we drove back across the river towards Vermont. Along the bridge, there were young couples, arms wrapped around each other, taking last looks in the crisp night air before they set forth into the real world and whatever it had to throw at them. There were also a few sets of parents, getting ready to see what would become of their children the graduates and possibly wondering what to do with the rest of their lives now that the kids were grown. I wondered which group of people Josie and I were most like, the young or the old.

————

AT JOSIE'S PLACE, STANDING OUTSIDE HER CAR, I GAVE HER A small Tupperware bin filled with her share of the loot. She smiled. Anyone watching would have thought I had brought some homemade cookies.

"Want to come in for a night cap?"

"Indeed, I do."

I did not spend that night at the Hotel Coolidge.

THIRTY-EIGHT

BACK IN NEW YORK, A FEW DAYS LATER, I PACKED UP ALL MY research and anything else tied to the Lessaker Museum job. There wasn't much of a paper trail, but there were a few supplies and leftover odds and ends. I bundled everything into a duffel bag and took the bus out to Clyde's place in Leonia.

Living outside the city, he had a house with a fireplace, which my apartment did not. Me alone, standing at a barbecue grill in an NYC public park, burning up a pile of evidence while not cooking any hot dogs would probably have gotten too much attention. And then I would have been hard-pressed to explain my cache of Lessaker-related documents so soon after the place was in the news. So Clyde agreed to let me use his fireplace.

He was cooking some burgers out on his backyard grill when I arrived, but he wouldn't let me burn any evidence there.

"It's going to mess with my smoky flavors," he said. "Paper doesn't burn right. I only put wood chips and charcoal in here."

He was standing in short pants and sandals, waving a large set of tongs at me and gesturing at his grill.

"After we eat this gourmet meal, you can make use of the fireplace."

We did not speak much about the job while we were outside, just to be safe. Instead we talked about vacation plans and bucket list trips we would probably never take. I wanted to see the Marquesas Islands. Clyde had a dream of visiting the pyramids in Egypt. Then Keisha said she had bought tickets to visit Antarctica, because she wanted to see it before it all melted.

This surprised me. She seemed smart enough not to make a lot of flashy purchases so soon after a big heist, and Clyde should have warned her against it as well.

"Did you spend *all* your money on that trip?" I asked.

She grinned.

Clyde started laughing. "You never told him, did you?"

"Told me what?"

"I sold ArtLocatr to some venture capitalists for a quarter million," she said.

"Our fake app?"

"I had some downtime in December, so I made it a real app. I made more from selling that than I did from the heist itself."

I laughed along with them. I guess I should have learned to be a computer programmer instead of a thief.

Keisha and I took the empty dishes inside while Clyde cleaned his grill. Once the dishwasher was loaded and running, we went into the living room and Clyde opened the flue. It was summer and probably a little too warm for a fire, but no one was going to convict us for robbing a museum on the basis of having used the fireplace in the summer.

I sat next to the hearth, loading in papers as we talked.

"I think you might be getting too old for this, Brady," Clyde said.

"Me? I feel as young as the day I was born."

"I'm worried about you out there, getting a gun pointed at you."

"They didn't shoot us."

"No, but at your age, you could have a heart attack, fast as a flier, just like that." He snapped his fingers to indicate how quickly he meant. "You don't eat very healthy to start with. Too much red meat."

"You just served me hamburgers, Clyde!"

"You should have asked for a veggie burger instead."

"Did you have veggie burgers you could have cooked for me?"

"Hell, no, that stuff's an abomination."

"You're *both* too old," Keisha said. "And you bicker like a couple of old biddies."

"Listen to this one," Clyde said. "She does *one* job and suddenly she thinks she's a criminal mastermind."

"Keisha was a great asset, Clyde. I'd be delighted to work with her again."

"Thank you," she said.

"Of course she's good, she's related to me! You can't spell 'genius' without the word 'gene.' But that don't mean she should sass talk her elders."

"Emphasis on *elders*," Keisha said with a laugh. "What's next, Brady? Are you going to rob the AARP?"

"That would be a big score. They're sitting on a lot of membership dues," I said. "But it's all digital money in a bank account. And I would not want to steal from desperate, frail old people, like Clyde here."

"I let you use my fireplace, but I'm the one getting burnt! This has turned into a roast, and somehow I'm the meat."

He went into the kitchen and came back with drinks for everyone.

"Actually," I said. "I'm thinking about giving up for real. Josie was offered a job in the city. If she moved down here, we could make another go of it. But I'd have to give up stealing."

Clyde and Keisha looked at each other and smiled.

"What?"

"You're going to retire, just like that?"

"I think it's sweet," Keisha said. "To give up what he loves for a woman."

"I don't love stealing things," I said. "It's just something I'm good at. I don't *need* to do it. At least, I don't think I do. I can get another regular job."

"Then I won't ask him," Keisha said to Clyde.

"Ask me what?"

"Nothing."

"Since she proved herself on this job, she thought you might want to partner up with her again on another job she found. But that was before we knew you were retired."

"What's the play?" I said.

"Don't tell him, Keisha. The man's swooning in the season of romance. We wouldn't want to interfere with his future."

"I didn't say I want in, I'd just like to know what kind of job it is."

"Alright. It's a school for international students. The Robert Van Wyck Preparatory Academy. The tuition is insanely high. Nobody questions it because private schools are already expensive. But this place has few facilities and not much staff. It's just one floor of a building in Midtown. A few classrooms."

"Doesn't seem like the kind of place rich people would send their kids," I said.

"Not if they want their children to get an education. The school is actually a money-laundering scheme—parents pay tuition from abroad, then get most of their money back in cash here. That way they can bypass currency importation laws and whatever restrictions their country has set up. Almost every country lets you send money overseas for education."

"Is this all digital money, though?"

"No, that's the trick of it. The school distributes money in cash to hide the paper trail. So after tuition payments come in, they convert it to green, and the Van Wyck Academy is like a bank without security."

I thought about it. Keisha had proven herself on the fake museum job. Her intel here seemed good. On the other hand, I was supposed to be getting out of the game.

"Josie wants me to stop stealing," I mused. "But she never said I couldn't take a job as a consultant."

THIRTY-NINE

THE DISCOVERY OF VERTIGO BY LOTTYE KUGEIOS, THE original, hangs in my bedroom, behind the door, so anyone who casually sticks their head in won't be able to see it. They'd have to come all the way in, lie down on the bed, and close the door to discover that it's there.

Josie had actually painted two copies of it, as a surprise. She thought I could keep one of the forgeries for myself. Keisha and I had noticed the extra fake during our Thanksgiving break-in, but in all the confusion and panic when the Russians showed up, I forgot to ask about it.

Then when we replaced the fakes with the real paintings on New Year's Eve, we must have accidentally hung the second duplicate in the Lessaker Museum instead of the original, which was still in the minivan.

After the authorities got involved, I could never find a safe time and place to switch it back, so I've been holding on to the real thing ever since.

I've come to love it.

Just before Thanksgiving, in the truck with Cesteroski's

henchman, I had said I would never pay a million dollars for any painting. But I've changed my mind. This one is worth it.

As I said, it's hidden behind the door in my bedroom, so for now, I'm the only one who ever sees it, the painting of the castle window and the gold mountain in the moonlight.

But in September, when she starts her job at Columbia, Josie will be able to see it too.

Milton Keynes UK
Ingram Content Group UK Ltd.
UKHW040728010823
426141UK00004B/243